"I have your baby, Mr. Hawksmoor."

Looking cuddly and sexy, Nate Hawksmoor peered at Hallie. "If you said you're having my baby, sweetheart, you've got the wrong apartment. If you said you want to have my baby—" he paused, scanning her flannel nightgown "—don't you think you should buy me dinner first?"

"I have no doubt that you have a far-ranging and lively sex life, Mr. Hawksmoor. Otherwise, I wouldn't be here now." Irritated with herself that she found him even the slightest bit appealing, she grabbed his shirtfront. "Come get your baby!"

Inside her apartment, she let him go. Pointing toward the baby, she said, "Merry Christmas. Now please take her home with you."

He flicked her a suspicious glance. "What the hell is this?"

"I'm guessing it's a baby," she said, unfolding a diaper.

"But I *can't* have a baby!" Nate protested.

She raised her eyebrows. "And how many years have you been celibate, Mr. Hawksmoor?"

"Okay, okay, so the possibility exists that it could be mine!"

"Look at this." Hallie waved Nate closer. "It's a birthmark—looks like a fleur-de-lis."

Nate knelt down, frowning. "Damn," he said with feeling.

Dear Reader,

Ho! Ho! Ho! 'Tis the season to be jolly, and Love & Laughter aims to be just that!

Popular Renee Roszel has written the first of our RIGHT STORK, WRONG ADDRESS books. You guessed it: the baby ends up at the wrong address. In this case, the heroine discovers the baby underneath her Christmas tree in *Gift-Wrapped Baby*. Definitely not what she asked Santa for—at least not until she meets the sexy father....

Stephanie Bond has had a stellar year with Love & Laughter, first writing the bestsellers #35 *KIDS Is a 4-Letter Word** and #37 *WIFE Is a 4-Letter Word**. She returns with the hilarious *Naughty or Nice?* It features a real Scrooge of a hero who learns the true meaning of Christmas. Moreover, he also discovers that sometimes being naughty is a lot more fun. You will also find Stephanie Bond writing for Temptation. *Club Cupid* will be on sale February 1999.

Enjoy your Christmas treats, and remember there are absolutely no calories in Love & Laughter!

Malle Vallik

Malle Vallik
Associate Senior Editor

*If you missed these treasures, you can order them from Harlequin Reader Service.
U.S.: 3010 Walden Ave., Buffalo, NY 14269.
Canada: P.O. Box 609, Fort Erie, Ontario L2A 5X3

GIFT-WRAPPED BABY
Renee Roszel

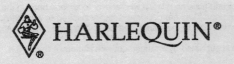

HARLEQUIN®

TORONTO • NEW YORK • LONDON
AMSTERDAM • PARIS • SYDNEY • HAMBURG
STOCKHOLM • ATHENS • TOKYO • MILAN • MADRID
PRAGUE • WARSAW • BUDAPEST • AUCKLAND

ISBN 0-373-44057-X

GIFT-WRAPPED BABY

Copyright © 1998 by Renee Roszel Wilson

A funny thing happened...

My birthday and wedding anniversary are both within a week of Christmas, so I fly from one festivity to another with great gusto. All the decorated stores, holiday parties and observances seem to be an extension of my personal celebrations—as though the whole world has joined in to share my happiness.

Because the season is so special, I love Christmas stories. I enjoy bringing to life the unique, seasonal warmth between loved ones at this exceptional time of getting together and making memories.

Gift-Wrapped Baby was a pleasure to write, because it turns two lonely strangers—however reluctant at the outset—into a family. I hope you are entertained by the antics of Hallie and Nate as a precious baby brings them together for a magical, merry Christmas.

Last but not least... "Happy Holidays" to all of you. I'd love to hear from readers, so write to me at:
P.O. Box 7001541, Tulsa, OK 74170.

—Renee Roszel

**To Animal Rescue Societies everywhere, and the folks
who work tirelessly to save abandoned and
abused critters.
And to Alex, a terrier mix, the newest member
of our family.**

1

THE TELEPHONE RANG, jarring Hallie awake. Opening one eye, she squinted at the bedside clock. Six-thirty on Christmas morning?

When the phone's high-pitched trill continued to trumpet through her brain, she scrambled to the edge of the bed and hefted the cordless receiver. "The building had better be on fire."

"Merry Christmas to you, too," chirped a familiar female voice.

Hallie yawned and pushed her hair out of her eyes. "Bea?" She grimaced. "I thought we were friends."

Laughter that sounded like rusty hinges made Hallie hold the phone away from her ear. "The kids were up at five, honeydew. For me it's the middle of the day."

"That's fascinating. Goodbye."

"Okay, okay, grumpy. I just wanted to wish you a Merry Christmas and tell you that if you change your mind about Christmas dinner, it'll be at two. That's plenty of time for you to drive from Tulsa to Bartlesville."

Hallie had to smile. Bea was a good friend, the only high school classmate she'd kept in touch with over the past eight years. "Thanks, but I need to catch up on some work." That was a lie, but it was kinder than admitting that seeing her friend with her children and husband would only make Hallie feel more alone. "You're great to call, though."

That squeaky laugh rang out. "Yeah, I could tell you were thrilled."

A sound caught Hallie's attention. Jingling. She cocked her head toward the bedroom door.

"Hallie?" Bea said. "You there?"

Hallie heard the faint sound again and stood. "Shush," she whispered, creeping to the door and peering out. From her vantage point she could see into the living room. Her Christmas tree came into view, its tinsel sparkling in the morning light. The sound jingled again. This time Hallie thought she detected movement beneath the tree.

Movement?

"Honeydew? Is everything okay?"

Hallie found herself crouching, then crawling one-handed. "I— Listen, Bea, I have to go—Merry Christmas…" She disconnected and dropped the phone, scrambling soundlessly across the hallway. She stopped at the entrance to the living room.

Lowering herself almost flat, she peered beneath the tree branches. Did she have a mouse in her apartment? And if she did, it was *not* supposed to be stirring! She swallowed, picturing a rodent running around all over her packages, knocking a jingling ornament with its long, disgusting tail. She made a face and felt crawly.

Jingle-jingle.

As she watched, transfixed, a tiny human hand— with five tiny human fingers—reached up to bat at the jingle bell ornament. Hallie gaped, too stunned to move or breathe. She could only stare wide-eyed, noting with disbelief that the little hand was connected to a chubby arm, protruding from a pink bundle among the gifts beneath her tree.

There hadn't been any pink bundles under her tree last night. She knew sometimes she got preoccupied with work, but surely she would have remembered a pink bundle. She jerked up to her knees. This wasn't a nasty, disgusting mouse—it was a tiny human person!

"A *baby?*" she breathed, experiencing a mixture of panic and awe. Somebody had left a human baby person under her Christmas tree?

Too unsteady to stand, she crawled across the living room, her gaze glued to the bundle. When she got to the tree, she stared. Why, it truly was a beautiful baby. The infant looked at her. The little face was so angelic, the blue eyes big and inquisitive. "Oh…" Hallie's nose tingled with the warning that she was getting ready to cry. "Oh, sweetie…"

Her insidious maternal instincts overrode her need to remain detached. Hadn't Hallie promised herself she would *never* fall in love with any other woman's baby, ever again?

But even as her logical side berated her mothering side, she lifted the infant into her arms. Cuddled her. Hallie reasoned that, wrapped in pink, with a big gold foil bow tied across her middle, the baby was probably a girl.

Tucked farther back beneath the tree was a plastic tote bag. Hallie fished it out and opened it, all the while her tiny charge simply stared up at her with wide, trusting eyes. At least the child didn't seem hungry. She couldn't have been here long.

Poking around in the bag, Hallie came up with a folded sheet of paper. Smoothing it open, she read.

Or at least she tried. The handwriting was practically illegible. One word looked vaguely like "Vanilla." A word further down was completely distinct, however. "Hawksmoor."

"Nathan Hawksmoor?" Hallie murmured, as it all began to come clear. She dropped the note in the bag and stroked the baby's cheek. "I think whoever left you didn't realize your daddy moved across the hall."

She couldn't help herself and kissed the pink cheek. She guessed the baby was about four months old. Her skin was warm and smelled of talcum. "I'd love to get to know you, little one, but I can't. I only know your daddy because I sublet this apartment from him. So, before I start going soft and goo-gooey, I'd better give him the news." She shook her head, but couldn't keep from smiling at the innocent bundle. "Does your daddy even know about you?"

The baby reached up, patted Hallie's chin and cooed, filling Hallie with a rush of maternal longing. She closed her eyes and got hold of herself. "No you don't, sweetie." Settling the child on the carpeting, she stood. "I can't do this again. I'm getting you out of here."

Mustering her resolve, she marched from her apartment. She didn't allow herself an instant of hesitation before she banged on Nathan Hawksmoor's door.

After an interminable minute when she heard no response, she banged again. "Mr. Hawksmoor?" she called. Luckily, this was only a six-apartment complex, with two apartments on each floor. All the other tenants were away for Christmas. At least her shouting wouldn't cause a lot of unwelcome attention. "Mr. Hawksmoor? Please answer your door." She banged again. "This is important!"

Nothing.

She knew he was home. She'd heard him come in late last night. Just as she raised her fist to bang a third time, the doorknob rattled. The man who opened the door looked groggy, his coffee-brown hair mussed. He seemed taller than she remembered. And more naked, wearing only sweatpants.

"Yes?" He gazed sleepily at her, his eyelids at half-mast.

"I have your baby, Mr. Hawksmoor."

He stilled in the act of dragging a sweatshirt on over his head. He peered at her, looking cuddly and sexy and way too amused for the degree of emergency. "If you said you're having my baby, sweetheart, you've got the wrong apartment. If you said you want to have my baby—" he paused, scanning her flannel nightgown "—don't you think you should buy me dinner first?"

His perusal of her floral nightclothes reminded her she was woefully underdressed. But that was hardly the issue, and hardly important, considering the situation. Distressed by the stimulating view of his bare chest, she flipped the sweatshirt sleeve dangling off his shoulder. "Would you mind putting that on, or are you planning to wear it as a tie?"

With a careless shrug that elicited a show of rippling muscle, he obliged. His casual attitude made it obvious he was unmoved by her news. Surely the man didn't have babies dropped off at his door—or what someone had *thought* was his door—on a daily basis, no matter how irresistible he looked in the morning. "Listen, Mr. Hawksmoor. I have your baby," she repeated sternly. "Her name's Vanilla and she's under my tree."

Once again he grinned crookedly and lounged against the doorjamb. "If Christmas morning riddles are a tradition in Denmark, or on Pluto, or wherever you're from, could we do it later? I just got to bed."

All that sexy grinning and seductive lazing around was getting on her nerves. She blurted, "I have no doubt that you have a far-ranging and lively sex life, Mr. Hawksmoor. Otherwise I wouldn't be here now." Irritated with herself that she found him even the slightest bit appealing, she grabbed his shirtfront. "Come get your baby!"

"Hey, this is kidnapping, sweetheart."

He didn't sound very unsettled. Evidently women dragging him into their apartments took up a huge chunk of his social schedule. "Try not to panic, Mr. Hawksmoor. I *don't* have designs on you."

Inside her apartment, she let him go and gave him a shove toward the tree. Pointing to the baby, she said, "Merry Christmas. Now please take her home with you."

His amusement vanished and he flicked her a suspicious glance. "What the hell is this?"

It was her turn to feel amused. "I'm guessing it's a baby."

He frowned. "Why are you showing it to me?"

Hallie's exhale had all the earmarks of a curse. She flung her arms up and marched over to the infant. Going down on her knees, she reached inside the tote bag to retrieve the letter. Jerking it out, she held it up. "Read this."

He didn't move, but when Hallie waved it, scowling, he slowly bent to pluck the note from her fingers. "What is it?"

"All I know is, it has your name on it, and that this was once your apartment."

He unfolded the sheet of typing paper. Vanilla made a whimpering sound, and Hallie looked at the child, her heart constricting. She was probably hungry, or wet. She hesitated to get involved, didn't want to have anything to do with caring for this irresistible heart magnet. She'd already lost three little girls who'd wrapped her around their chubby fingers. Her heart couldn't stand for it to happen again.

The whimpering grew louder. With great regret, Hallie watched herself remove the ribbon and undo pink bunting to check the baby's diaper. "Wet," she mumbled.

"But I *can't* have a baby!" Nate wadded the note.

Hallie looked up as she pulled a fresh diaper from the bag. "And how many years have you been celibate, Mr. Hawksmoor?"

He scowled at her. "When my wife ran off, I didn't know she was pregnant."

"Ah." Hallie slipped off the old diaper. "So the celibacy thing's a bust, huh?"

"Okay, okay, so the possibility exists that it could be mine!"

"Why do you think she never told you?" Hallie asked. "And why didn't she ask for child support?"

He shrugged. "Viv got a nice inheritance from her grandfather a few weeks before she ran off. That was fourteen months ago. In her contorted little mind, she probably thought *I'd* ask for support if she kept in touch." Tossing the letter to the rug, he went on. "When she sent the divorce papers to my lawyer, I signed them. That was that."

"So you never knew you were going to be a papa, and she never knew you'd moved?"

"I'm not so sure I'm a papa." His jaw worked. "According to that note, she's found herself a new guy who's not crazy about raising another man's kid. It could be an excuse not to take responsibility for his own handiwork."

"Whichever—he sounds like a prince." Hallie readied the new diaper. She saw something on Vanilla's hip and stopped. Turning the baby slightly, she could see a red birthmark about the diameter of a nickel. "Look at this." She waved Nate to come closer.

"What?" He sounded dubious, as though he feared she'd discovered a second baby.

"Birthmark. It looks like a fleur-de-lis."

He knelt, frowning. "Damn."

Hallie stared at him. "What's the matter?"

He sat on the floor, looking a little pale. "Nothing."

Hallie scanned the red mark again and had a revelation. She eyed him. "You have one, too."

He peered at her but didn't speak.

She couldn't help but grin. "You have a fleur-de-lis on your butt, too? How cute."

He was grinding his teeth; she could tell by the way his jaws worked.

"That probably generates a lot of laughs in the locker room, huh—Daddy?" Why she enjoyed this, she had no idea. Maybe because not many minutes ago this handsome stud had managed to embarrass her with only a casual grin. And now, because of the telltale birthmark, he could hardly deny his fatherhood. All of a sudden he had a baby daughter he was expected to raise, and it was going to screw up his social life royally.

The baby whimpered, and Hallie remembered what she was supposed to be doing. "Okay, Vanilla, honey. I'm sorry."

"Her name is *not* Vanilla," he huffed. "Viv might be a latter-day flower child but she wouldn't have named a child 'Vanilla.'"

"Well, what did she name her? You figure it out."

The baby's whimpering grew stronger. Hallie put on the new diaper, folded the pink blanket around her and handed her to her father. "Here you go. Have a nice life." She grabbed the tote bag and dropped the wadded letter inside. Standing, she held it out. He would have to be as thick as the Great Wall of China to mistake her meaning.

Nate looked at her. She noticed his eyes were the same light blue as the baby's, but his lashes were long and dark, not blond like Vanilla's. "What do you expect me to do with it?" he asked, holding the pink bundle at arm's length as though it were radioactive.

"Take her home."

He looked as shocked as if she'd told him to eat it. "I can't take care of a baby."

"Of course you can." The baby was really crying now and Hallie found herself torn. Did she allow this…this inept *male* to take this baby home? Maybe he could make babies, but he had no inkling of what to do when faced with the responsibility of his creation.

The infant's cries had become choking wails of agony. Clearly she was starving to death and any delay would be murder most foul—at least in Vanilla's opinion. "Oh—give her to me!" Hallie took the baby and cuddled her to her chest. "Dig out one of those bottles and a can of formula. We'll have to heat it up."

"We?"

She drew herself up to her full, threatening five-four. "Yes, *we!*" Unfortunately for her threatening ability, she was a foot shorter than he. "You're the father. I'm only the neighbor."

"But I don't know what to do with it."

"First, Vanilla is not an it!"

"It's not Vanilla!"

"Well, whatever flavor she is, she's not an it!" Lifting the baby to her shoulder, she patted her back. "Get a bottle and that formula." Hallie heaved a sigh at her weakness. "I'll show you how to heat it. Then I want you to go."

His handsome face displayed a small measure of relief. "Thanks." He knelt and retrieved one of the two bottles and a can of formula. "I appreciate this—uh…"

She glanced at him, frowning. Good grief, he didn't even remember her name—which had been on her rent check every month for the past half year. "Hallie," she shouted over the baby's bellowing. "Hallie St. John."

"Right." He held out the formula and the bottle. "Now what, Hallie St. John?"

With a wayward rush of pity for the good-looking guy who'd just had his life turned upside down, Hallie led him to the kitchen.

Thirty minutes later Nate Hawksmoor and Vanilla were still there—much to Hallie's consternation. But her Christmas-spirit-neighborly-maternal side was winning out big-time over her get-them-out-of-here-that-baby-is-not-my-business rational side.

Her tummy full and her bottom dry, the baby slept on the couch, looking like a Christmas angel. Nate lounged on the floor, sipping fresh coffee and leaning against an easy chair. Hallie'd berated herself the entire time she'd made the coffee, but it had done no good. She'd still offered him a cup, and he'd accepted—no gigantic surprise. Deflated, she watched as he scanned his wife's badly penned, rumpled note. "I'm pretty sure," he began, taking a sip from his mug, "her name is not Vanilla Porterhouse Hawksmoor."

"Thank heaven."

He half grinned, but without humor. "The closest I can come is Vivienne Patricia. Vivienne was my wife's name. Patricia was her mother's." He shook his head. "The baby's named after my airhead ex-wife and Tyrannosaurus Rex Woman. Great start."

He glanced at Hallie, and she was glad she'd taken the time to change into jeans and a bulky sweater. Those eyes could do things—weird things—that made you want to check yourself just to make sure you hadn't thrown off all your clothes. Luckily her jeans zipper tended to stick. She cleared her throat. What were they talking about? Oh, right, Tyrannosaurus Rex Woman—his ex-mother-in-law. Baby names. "Well, if you don't like Vivienne or Viv..."

His mouth took on an unpleasant twist.

"Okay, what about Pat or Patty or Patsy?" She wondered what in the world she was doing, lounging on the floor with a man who was hardly more than a stranger, discussing baby names on Christmas morning. Why was she getting involved?

Because he's a helpless male, and you're a stupid nincompoop! her brain chided. Unfortunately, she found herself agreeing wholeheartedly with her brain, but unable to do a thing about it.

"Nope."

She frowned, confused. She'd lost the thread of conversation again.

"I've had girlfriends with those names. Seems kinky."

She closed her eyes, counting to ten. "Look, there aren't that many variations on Patricia. Maybe it would be faster if you tell me the names of women you haven't slept with, or we might *have* to call her Vanilla."

He sat close to the Christmas tree. Hallie couldn't understand why she was sitting cross-legged on the floor, facing him. If she was bright, she'd be behind one of the chairs, brandishing a whip, screaming, "Out! Out, Simba! Out!" As a poor substitute, she held her coffee mug in both hands in front of her, a shield of sorts.

He eyed her narrowly. "I didn't say I'd slept with them all."

Luckily this time she managed to recall what they'd been talking about and answered without any significant hesitation. "Sure."

He smirked at her. "You have a low opinion of me, don't you, Miss St. John?"

She sipped her coffee, stalling. She tried not to have any opinion of him. He was her landlord—the tall, good-looking man who smelled like cedar and cherry tobacco, a nice combination in an aftershave. Over the past six months she'd seen him bring two or three different women back to his apartment. The latest girlfriend was a curvy blonde who giggled a lot.

That's all she knew about him, other than that he was an architect who sometimes worked out of his apartment. She also worked at home, doing the book-keeping for several companies. Every so often they ran into each other in the hallway, where he'd leave his lingering cedar-tobacco scent and she'd sniff for a second or two longer than necessary. "I have no opinion, whatsoever, about you."

He grunted as though he didn't believe that. "You don't like me one bit."

She glanced at his face. He was grinning for the first time since he'd found out he was a father. Apparently he got a real charge out of her supposed aversion.

"You think I'm a sex-crazed maniac," he added.

She stared. Did he read minds? She took another sip of coffee, deciding to keep her mouth shut.

He shrugged. "Well, I'm not."

She arched a brow.

"I'm not."

"I don't really care, Mr. Hawksmoor."

"Call me Nate."

"Nate, I don't really care."

He downed the remainder of his coffee. "I think I'll have some more of that." He got up and went into the kitchen. "You make good coffee, Hallie."

"I know, Nate."

He came back. "You don't have to call me Nate every time you say anything."

"Thanks, Nate."

He chuckled; the sound was pleasant. "You're welcome, Hallie."

She felt her lips twitch, but she squelched the urge to enjoy his banter. *Don't let this guy get to you, Hallie. He's trying to soften you up, to ask you to help him with the baby. Don't let him suck you in!*

He joined her on the carpet, this time, nearer. She could detect his scent, mixed with the pine of her tree. She swallowed, lifting her mug so she could smell only coffee.

"What are your plans for today, Hallie?"

She bit her lip. Darn, why wasn't she in Bartlesville with Bea and her family? She put down her mug and toyed with one of the packages beneath her tree. "Oh, uh…I need to catch up on some work." She avoided his gaze.

"Mmm."

Unable to stop herself, she eyed him with suspicion. "Why?"

His glance held hers as he sipped coffee. When he lowered his mug he shrugged. "Do you have any more ideas about what we could call the baby?"

We? She didn't like the sound of we! "At least you're not calling her 'it' anymore," she mumbled, before a totally-out-of-nowhere thought struck. "Hey, have you ever dated a Trisha?"

He pursed his lips. "Nope."

"Do you like the name?"

"Trisha Hawksmoor," he murmured, as though testing it on the tongue. After a moment he nodded. "Yeah. I do."

She sighed. "Thank goodness that's over." Standing, she gave him a now-you-can-go nod, desperate to get him and his new daughter out of her apartment—and her life.

His smile was dazzling and a little too confident, filling her with dismay.

2

"DON'T YOU DARE look at me like that," she warned, taking a cautious step away.

"Like what?" His smile didn't fade.

She set her mug on the coffee table. "You know 'like what.' You think I'll break down and help you with Trisha. Well, you're dead wrong! I took care of my three stepsisters for ten years, and I don't intend to get involved with anybody else's kids ever again. Is that clear?"

His expression changed somehow, his eyes taking on a glow that exclaimed, "I'm saved! She knows how to take care of children! She'll take care of Trisha!"

"I will not!"

Trisha whimpered. Hallie realized she'd shouted, and winced. "I won't!" she insisted. "Just because she was under my tree does not make her my responsibility."

"I believe there's an old Chinese saying about that."

She eyed him dubiously. "I'm not interested."

"Aw, Hallie," he coaxed, his grin debilitating. "Where's your Christmas spirit? I'm not asking for much. Just a little help getting started."

Trisha whimpered again, and Hallie glanced at the

baby. The little darling was sucking on her fingers, acting fretful.

"What's wrong?" Nate asked.

"I don't know. She shouldn't be hungry or wet." Forgetting her desire to get rid of the Hawksmoor clan, she knelt beside the sofa and felt the baby's forehead. "No fever. I don't think she's sick."

"Maybe there's a pin sticking in her. I've heard to check for pins."

Hallie couldn't help smiling. "She's wearing a disposable diaper. They don't have pins." When he moved to stand beside her, she glanced up at him. "But that's a good sign. You're starting to think like a father."

His brows rose in a shrug of sorts. "A clueless one."

Hallie turned toward the baby to hide a renewed grin and took Trisha's fingers out of her mouth. She rubbed her thumb across the baby's lower gums. "Ah, I feel it."

"What?"

"A tooth." She stood and faced Nate. "Congratulations, she's teething."

"Is that good?"

Hallie smirked at his ignorance. "It's a pain, actually—for everybody concerned." She headed to her tree and scooped up a package, handing it to him. "Merry Christmas. I keep a few extra gifts in case somebody unexpected drops by." As if *that* was likely, she thought ruefully.

Clearly confused, Nate took the small box.

Confusion looked good on him, with those dark brows converging over sky-blue eyes.

When he only stared at her, she tapped the box. "Open it."

"This had better be an inflatable nanny."

She shook her head at him. "Keep dreaming, bachelor boy."

He peeled away the bright holiday wrapping to find a small white bakery box. Opening it, his perplexed expression didn't ease. "Cookies?"

"They're my homemade chocolate biscotti." She took one out and knelt beside the couch, pressing it into Trisha's hand. Immediately the baby stuck one end in her mouth and gummed it. Her fretful whimpering ceased.

"See?" Hallie stood, smiling with triumph. "Miracle."

Nate's glance went from his daughter's contented demeanor to Hallie's face. He flashed another one of those heart-stopping grins. "You really know about kids." He closed the biscotti box with what looked like reverence. "I owe you one, Hallie St. John."

She gazed into those arresting eyes and felt herself weakening in her stance to keep out of Trisha's life. Suddenly resigned to the fact that she couldn't send this novice out into the cold, cruel world of child-rearing totally unprepared, she hefted the tote bag and held it out. "You take this." She scooped up the baby, cuddling her close. "I'll help get you started."

After all, Christmas was going to be lonely, with nothing for company but memories of her young stepsisters, now halfway across the country. Getting Nate's daughter settled in would take her mind off being alone. But that was all she planned to do. "I'm not taking on your baby, mind you," she warned. "It's today and today only." She walked to her door, then turned back. "And you'll owe me a lot more than *one*, Mr. Hawksmoor."

He winked, making it plain he'd felt all along he could break down her resistance. Darn him and his helpless-new-daddy appeal. Hallie fought the urge to kick him in his fleur-de-lis.

As NATE OPENED his apartment door, he heard Hallie gasp. "Oh, my Lord."

He fought a grin at her reaction to his girlfriend's creativeness. Buffy had decorated his apartment to within an inch of its life. There was tinsel upon tinsel. Diminutive Christmas villages littered every surface. Mistletoe hung from so many places one would have thought the parasite was sucking the apartment building dry of its innards.

Candy canes dangled from greenery strung around every doorway, snaking along walls to loll on the mantel and occasional tables, then dripping to drag on the floor. Groupings of candles huddled everywhere—squat ones, skinny ones, tall ones, glitter-covered ones—mixed and mingled with glass ornaments and gold-painted pinecones. Even the throw pillows were wrapped in holiday ribbon. "Like it?" he queried.

She glanced at him, her gaze wide with horror. For the first time he noticed her eyes were hazel. An awful word for such a pretty color.

"You're a cinch for the cover of *Tacky Home and Garden*," she muttered.

He hefted a brow. "You're insulting my girl-friend." He didn't want to admit that he half agreed with Hallie, but Buffy had been so industrious he'd hated to dampen her enthusiasm. She was nothing if not enthusiastic. "I like a woman who does homey things for her man."

Hallie's eyes grew bigger and flashed. "Oh, Lord. You're one of those." It came out somewhere between a groan and a sneer.

"One of those what?"

"Those men who have to be the boss and who think a woman's place is in the home, barefoot and pregnant."

He closed his door and leaned against it. She was right—except for the barefoot part—but why did it sound like a felony when she said it? "And I gather you're one of those women who has to emasculate a man to feel fulfilled."

She glowered at him. "I thought you wanted my help."

He felt the slap of her remark and decided he'd better keep his feelings about pushy, opinionated women to himself. He knew he was treading on thin ice with her as it was. "Sorry," he said as mildly as his irritation would allow. "I do want your help, Hallie. I'm a little tense. Remember, I just became a father." He indicated the baby in her arms. "So, what do we do first?"

Trisha continued to gnaw on the biscotti, her big blue gaze following the sound of their voices. When he spoke, the baby's glance shifted to stare at her daddy. He went still, watching her watch him. She had a cleft in her chin, just like his. He'd never thought of tiny babies having clefts in their chins. It didn't seem like such a little face would have room.

"What are you looking at?" Hallie interrupted his train of thought.

He snapped his gaze to hers. "Nothing. Just... looking."

Hallie smiled. When she chose to be pleasant, she did it well. He smiled back. "She's beautiful, Nate." Her smile faded, as though she'd caught herself, remembering her plans to remain aloof. "Where's your bedroom? We'll make a temporary bed for her in there."

After emptying a drawer in Nate's dresser, they made Trisha a respectable little bed. Holding a gooey half-gummed biscotti in her baby fingers, Trisha fell asleep. Hallie tugged the sticky cookie from her hand and pulled the curtains, motioning Nate out of the room.

Once the door was closed, she said, "Okay, let's get this junk out of here."

"What junk?"

She gestured broadly, indicating the room. "This Christmas junk. The first lesson you might as well learn is that babies stick things in their mouths. Before you know it, Trisha will be crawling, and you don't want her sucking down a lot of dusty bric-a-brac."

He didn't have a problem with dismantling the decorations, but he had a feeling his girlfriend would. "Buffy's coming over this afternoon."

Hallie headed into the kitchen. "Good, she can help. Where do you keep your trash bags?"

By the time the Four-Star-General Pain From Across The Hall was finished, Nate had nothing left to indicate it was Christmas, except the small plastic tree perched on his dining room table.

He frowned as Hallie stuffed the last of the greenery into a garbage bag, but he had to admit she worked like a Trojan. He also had to admit another hard truth—for a jackbooted, militant Trojan, she had a cute tush.

Realizing there was no future in admiring the tush of a female tyrant, he shifted his gaze away and forced himself to keep his mouth shut about the liberties she was taking with his property. He needed her help, damn it. Any other time he wouldn't have put up with such high-handedness from a woman, but to be suddenly thrust into the role of a father, he was out of his element and he knew it. For his daughter's sake, he held his tongue.

Hallie stood, drawing his attention. She swept her hand through her short, dark blond hair, looking more like a pixie than some dictator's henchman. He knew all too well that looks could be deceiving. Unfortunately, beggars couldn't be choosers, and right now he needed Hallie's assistance. "Buffy's going to freak," he warned.

Hallie finished twist-tying the bag and brushed her bangs out of her eyes to better scowl at him. "What does she do when she freaks, giggle more?"

He eyed her with curious amusement. "Have you been spying on me and my female friends?"

Her face went pink and she broke eye contact. Hefting the bag, she held it out. "Put this someplace."

"Yes, Sir. General, Sir." He hoisted the bag over a shoulder and saluted. "Any further orders, Sir?"

She pressed her hands to the small of her back and stretched. "We have to buy some stuff."

"On Christmas Day?"

She wiped her brow with her forearm. "Babies

need more formula and diapers in one day than your wife left.''

"Ex-wife."

"Whatever. But we have to get to a store. Unless you think little Trisha's overweight and would benefit from a bad case of diaper rash.''

Nate exhaled wearily. That was just like Viv. Do it halfway or don't do it at all. "What's diaper rash?"

Hallie eyed the ceiling. "Trust me. You don't want it, and neither does Trisha."

Hell, what he didn't know about babies would make a fairly hilarious sitcom. He checked his watch. One o'clock. Man, this day was dragging. "Buffy should be here anytime. She's bringing leftover turkey dinner from her family's."

Hallie held up her hands, looking unimpressed. "Wash?"

He nodded toward the kitchen.

"Why didn't you eat Christmas dinner with your girlfriend's family?" She headed into the kitchen.

He followed. "Meeting a woman's family means more commitment than I'm willing to give."

At the sink, Hallie glanced his way. "Is that what you told her?"

His bossy, mouthy neighbor was sharp. He grinned in spite of his personal feelings about her. "I told her I had to work."

Hallie soaped her hands, dropping her gaze. "Don't you have any family here?"

"My brother. But he and his wife spend Christmas with her family—which I wouldn't wish on a rabid dog."

She glanced his way, but didn't respond.

"And you?" He opened the rear door to the apartment and tossed the trash into a Dumpster a floor below. She soaped for another moment before he prodded, ''Hallie?''

Finally, she lay the soap in its dish. ''My father is on his third wife. Mr. Control Freak. He lives in town, but we aren't close. My stepsisters have moved to Washington state, with a new daddy. They sent me a present.'' She swallowed, and he sensed great sadness. So those three little girls were the family she wished she was spending the holidays with. ''A friend invited me to her house, but I—I...'' She shook her head as she tore off a paper towel and dried her hands.

''You told your friend you had to work,'' he guessed.

She wadded the towel and checked under the sink, finding the wastebasket. When she met his gaze, she finger-combed her hair out of her eyes. ''Do you think your girlfriend would watch Trisha while we go to the store? It would only be about twenty minutes.''

Nate thought it was interesting how she'd side-stepped his question. It seemed she didn't want to be comparable to him, even in a small lie about how she was spending Christmas.

As for *her* question, he had no idea how Buffy might feel about baby-sitting. He'd only been dating her for the past month; the subject of babies hadn't come up. He didn't even know if Buffy had younger brothers and sisters. It made him wonder what in hell they spent their time talking about. He started to speak, but the doorbell interrupted. With a nod, he indicated the exit to the living room. ''Why don't we find out?''

''Would you trust her with Trisha?''

"She's never come after me with a hatchet, if that's what you mean."

At the door, Hallie passed him a jaundiced look. "That's not what I mean. Does she know anything about children?"

He shrugged, annoyed by her cross-examination. "How in blazes would I know?"

She shook her head, apparently concluding his relationships with women were one hundred percent physical. As if it were her business! "There are a few skills I don't require in a date, Miss St. John," he said under his breath. "But next time, just for you, I'll give a written exam."

Her glance sharpened, but she had no time to respond before he swung open the door.

FOR SHOPPERS, pickings were slim on Christmas Day. Hallie was grateful a nearby Grab-And-Go carried baby food and disposable diapers. They could make do until tomorrow.

Tomorrow? She closed her eyes, experiencing a rush of dread. She'd never thought about prolonging this ordeal beyond today. Maybe Buffy would take over for her. After all, she was his girlfriend. Baby-sitting was more a girlfriend's job than a neighbor's.

On their way back, Hallie sat in Nate's two-seater sports car, recalling the curvy Buffy as she'd stood at Nate's door, a big basket of leftover Christmas dinner in her arms.

She was about Hallie's height, but had to weigh twenty pounds more in chest volume alone. Her hair was the same dark blond shade as Hallie's, but Buffy's hairdo must have been copied right off the latest cover of *Cosmo*. Scraggly but chic, swept back in a hair clip, with strategic wisps dangling in her pretty face. Buffy's white, off-the-shoulder sweater made it clear she was braless. Paired with slinky silk slacks, her attire didn't exactly shout "I'm here to baby-sit."

Though Hallie hadn't been privy to "the many moods of Buffy," she'd recognized the disgruntled look of a woman whose plans to get naked had been dashed by the presence of not only a baby but another woman.

It had been fascinating to watch Nate charm his girlfriend into baby-sitting. It hadn't surprised Hallie when Buffy had started to giggle and simper and coo that she was *delighted* to help. The Me-Tarzan-You-Jane game was painful to witness. She stifled a shiver.

"You know," she said, her voice sounding overly loud in the tense stillness. "You'll have to get a bigger car."

She could feel his eyes on her. "This has two seats."

She glanced over, barely able to see him, drowning as she was in packages. "Air bags have killed children in the front passenger seat, but how you deal with your child's safety is none of my business. Have it your way."

He flicked her a narrowed glance, but didn't speak. She watched his jaw work as her cautionary words sank in. This baby was changing his life quickly and drastically. Though he might be unwilling to admit it yet, he was coming to the sad conclusion that one of those drastic changes meant his cherry-red "babe mobile" would have to go.

She felt a tug of sympathy. The poor control-freak hunk had suffered a severe dose of parental reality in a very short time. She doubted that many single men—or single women for that matter—would be any more amenable to such life-altering events than he'd been.

Not another word was said as they unloaded baby supplies and took the stairs to the second floor. That was okay with Hallie. After all, she wasn't involved in this thing to make a buddy or cultivate a lover. She was simply doing a good deed for Christmas, and the sooner she could get back to her own life, the better.

Even before Nate unlocked his door, they were hit by the sound of wailing.

"Oh, dear." Hallie rushed in and dumped her packages on the leather sofa that faced the hearth. "It's that dratted tooth again."

She ran to the bedroom, but skidded to a halt at the open door. Trisha wasn't in her makeshift bed. Whirling, she glowered, worried and confused, then realized the sound was coming from the kitchen. "Buffy?"

"We're in here." The buxom baby-sitter didn't sound happy.

Hallie beat Nate into the kitchen by one step. She stumbled to a stop when she saw the scene in front of her. An instant later Nate collided with Hallie, making her stumble.

"What the…" he muttered.

Grasping Hallie's upper arms, he steadied her. But she didn't need steadying as much as she needed restraining. She wanted to kill Buffy. Yanking herself from Nate's grasp, she stalked toward the woman, anger rising in her like volcanic lava.

Buffy had propped Trisha in a semi-sitting position on a pillow in a kitchen chair. Both baby and pillow were tied to the chair by a green terry-cloth belt, probably from Nate's bathrobe. The belt was knotted at her chest to keep her from toppling to her face. But that was only the beginning of Buffy de Sade's torture.

There were splotches of bright rouge on Trisha's cheeks. Her lips were an even brighter shade of red. Her ash-blond brows were heavily penciled in dark brown. Her tiny fingernails and toenails were painted a lustrous black. Buffy sat facing Trisha, holding a lipstick in one hand and an eyeliner brush in the other.

"Oh—my—dear—*Lord!*" Hallie rushed to the baby and began fumbling with the knot at her chest. "She looks like a teensy bald streetwalker about to be autopsied." After tossing away the belt, Hallie swept a bawling Trisha into her arms and glared at Buffy. "What do you think you're doing?"

Buffy's expression was pinched in annoyance. She slammed down the makeup and stood. "Well, naturally, I was trying to get her to stop crying. I figured, getting all prettied up made me feel better, so—"

Hallie's feral groan stopped Buffy in midsentence. She was so angry with the nincompoop woman, she couldn't respond for fear she'd go insane and chew off her face. She whirled away. Stalking to Nate, she gave him a look that she hoped made her murderous feelings clear about girlfriends who were so simple-minded that they thought the way to handle a sobbing infant was to give them a makeover.

His features were closed in a scowl. She couldn't tell if he was upset to see his baby daughter made up like a ten-dollar harlot or if he was irked by Hallie's shrewishness.

"I'll get her cleaned up," she shouted, cradling the

squalling baby against her chest. "It should take about fifteen minutes."

Grabbing the front of his sweatshirt, she tugged him out of the kitchen. "The next time you look for a girlfriend—" she muttered. "Shop somewhere besides Airheads-R-Us!"

3

THIS CHRISTMAS DAY had been vastly different than Hallie could have imagined. And it wasn't over yet.

She lay her dish towel aside and passed through the dining area to Nate's living room. He sat on the leather sofa in front of a cozy fire. Trisha lay in his arms, sucking on her bottle. The lights were low, and Hallie had to lean over to make out the baby's face. Her eyes were closed. The little darling was asleep. Smiling, Hallie gently coaxed the bottle from Nate's hand.

He looked up and she pressed a finger to her lips. Placing the bottle on the coffee table, she lifted the baby from his arms, mouthing, "I'll put her to bed."

Trisha had had an exhausting afternoon, what with the tooth she was cutting, and Buffy. In trying to pacify her, Nate had gone through most of the box of biscotti. Hallie hoped Trisha was so exhausted she'd sleep through the night. Nate looked as if he could use a break.

When she returned to the living room she slumped on the sofa, beside him. She knew she should give him a crisp salute and exit his life, but she figured Nate had questions. As a daddy, he was still awfully green.

"Well," she began, brushing aside her bangs, "how do you think it went?"

He draped an arm across the back of the sofa, his fingers grazing her shoulder. She moved away from the touch; it was an automatic reaction, a defense mechanism she'd built up against authoritative men. He seemed to sense her disinclination and shifted his hand away.

She realized his light touch on her shoulder had been complete happenstance. He hadn't been making a sexual overture. There was nothing sensual going on between them. They were absolutely not each other's type. Which was good. She didn't need her landlord coming on to her, making her life more complicated.

"She's still alive," he said, and Hallie had to search around in her brain for what she'd asked. Oh, right, she'd wanted to know how he'd thought it went. She smiled at his joke, though she would have preferred not to find him amusing.

"Being alive after the first day is a good start," she joked, relaxing a bit.

"Thanks for fixing dinner. It was good."

She shrugged off the compliment. "Hey, with a pound of hamburger, I can do anything."

"And thanks for the lesson about feeding her that creamed cereal."

She glanced away, unaccustomed to being complimented. She'd cared for her three stepsisters for years with hardly a "good for you" from either her father or her stepmother. Deciding the subject could use changing, she voiced something that had been on her mind. "You have nice things." Though his apartment was sparsely furnished, the pieces were well built, of mellow wood, rich textiles, and polished leather.

Wholly unlike the pale green and mauve vinyls, blond wood and glass that outfitted her furnished apartment.

"Thanks," he said.

She faced him, curious. "How is it that your taste changed so drastically from the time you lived in my apartment?"

He grinned, but without humor. "In a weak moment, I let Viv furnish the place."

Hallie glanced at the fire and inhaled the scent of wood smoke. "Some people would call that impulse nice, not weak."

"Yeah, sure," Nate said, drawing her gaze.

There was that control-freak personality rearing its ugly head again. Even the distant memory of relinquishing a little control apparently grated on him. "Besides, I thought you were the guy who liked women who did homey things. I imagine decorating the apartment would fall into that category."

He glanced her way, arching a brow. He'd heard the sarcasm. Without a word, he rose to his feet and Hallie had a feeling he was about to grab her by the scruff of the neck and toss her out on her sarcastic backside. "Want some coffee?" he asked.

Startled to find herself still on the sofa and not sprawled in the hallway, she nodded. While he was in the kitchen, she cleared her throat, searching for her voice and wondering why she'd nodded "yes." She really needed to get the heck out of his apartment and his life. Even though there were no sexual vibrations between them in the slightest, she had to admit he had a certain raw allure...for a domineering male.

When he came back with two steaming mugs of coffee, she accepted with a rather scratchy "Thanks."

He didn't smile, but nodded. "You'd have thought

a guy like me would insist his woman run on out and get coffee—and do it barefoot.''

She eyed him with suspicion. ''Except for one small detail.''

''What's that?''

''*I* don't happen to be your woman.''

He took a sip of coffee, watching her over the rim of his mug. She was startled by how attractive those blue eyes were in the glimmer of the fire. And the way the light hit his hair gave it a coppery glow. He had long lashes, so long, in fact, that the mere possession of them ought to be a crime. Men should have short, stubby lashes and leave the long, thick ones for…well—*her.* Life could be wildly unfair.

He set his mug on the coffee table. ''Thanks for making that clear, but I'd already sensed you aren't my woman,'' he said. ''I figured I owe you for today, so I forced myself to get the coffee.''

Though there was a teasing edge to his voice, she knew not to be drawn in by his charm. He'd already made it unapologetically clear he was a male chauvinist pig and proud of it. ''Well, aren't you the Renaissance man,'' she quipped.

His brows dipped. She could tell he wasn't accustomed to women kidding him—at least not without sexual overtones. She decided it would be best to keep the conversation on business. ''Do you have any questions?''

He relaxed back, but continued to watch her. ''Yeah.''

''Shoot.'' This was better. Keep their intercourse—er, dialogue centered on the baby. That's why she was there—to get this studly bachelor started on his journey into fatherhood.

"Do you hate all men, or just me?"

She was so taken aback by the unexpected question, she almost spit out her coffee. Stunned, she thumped down her mug. *"Excuse me?"*

"I said, do you hate—"

"I heard what you said," she cut in. "And of course I don't hate all men."

"Just me, then."

"I don't hate you, Mr. Hawksmoor," she said, fairly sure her stiffened posture shouted, "Can't you see I'm crazy about you! That's why I've stuffed myself into the corner, as far away from you as I can get and still be on the same sofa."

Appearing thoughtful, he reached for his coffee mug. After a taste, he glanced her way. "Whatever." He put down his mug, and she had a feeling he didn't believe her. But it also seemed clear it didn't much matter to him.

She straightened her shoulders. "When I asked for questions, I meant about Trisha."

"I know." He flashed a grin.

She frowned. "You're a very frustrating man."

"You're a bossy female."

She grinned, without a single inkling why. Maybe this good-natured antagonism was the best direction for their relationship to take. "I bet your girlfriend thinks Dr. Spock is that pointy-eared character on 'Star Trek.'"

"I bet you think you're funny."

"I think I'm a laugh a minute." She shook her head, recalling Buffy's paint job on Trisha that afternoon. Errant amusement gurgled in her throat.

He leaned forward, resting his elbows on his knees, eyeing her, his lips quirking. "Buffy was upset with you. Tearing down her decorations and yelling at her." Hallie heard rumbling in his chest. As she watched, the rumble billowed into rich full-fledged laughter. "Good Lord, what she did to that poor baby."

Hallie felt guilty about her outburst that afternoon. Sometimes her flash-fire temper got the better of her and she'd been trying to figure out a way to apologize. But with his laughter, she could no longer contain her own. "It really was *not* funny," she insisted.

"No." He chuckled. "It was pretty bad."

"Promise me you won't let Buffy baby-sit again?"

His eyes glittered with mirth. "Only when the cops need extras for a lineup of baby hookers."

Hallie exploded with giggles, her eyes beginning to water. "Or if Trisha especially requests to be tied to a chair."

The warmth of his laughter echoed in the room, and the sight of his grin sent a thrill along her spine. Darn, this gorgeous hunk of male could be a lot of fun.

Hallie felt niggling misgivings. She was starting to enjoy Mr. Wrong, way too much. Jumping up, she squelched her amusement and worked for a serious expression. "Well, Mr. Hawksmoor..." She cleared a wayward giggle from her throat. "It's been an interesting Christmas, but I think I'll call it a night." She swept her bangs out of her eyes. "Good luck with—everything."

He continued to grin, but the laughter vanished from his gaze, replaced by surprise. He got up from the sofa. "Oh...right." He seemed momentarily uncertain, as though he'd suddenly realized Trisha was his and his alone from now on. Though his smile had dimmed, it was still striking. "Thanks, again." Walking with her, he opened the door. "Good night, Hallie."

She felt curiously awkward at his nearness and stuck out a hand more as a barrier than a polite offering. "Good night."

He glanced at her hand and then at her face. With a little smile, he took her fingers in his. "Merry Christmas."

His hand was large and warm. She liked the way he shook hands, which was the silliest thought she'd had in…well, forever! Besides, he wasn't actually shaking her hand. Just holding it. Holding it so…so…disturbingly. Why did such a simple gesture of civility seem like a sex act? Pulling free, she mumbled, "Merry Christmas," and scurried to her apartment.

Once safely inside, she sagged against the door and closed her eyes. Her heart pounded in a peculiar, rapid staccato. Weird. It must be Nate's coffee. He probably didn't use decaffeinated.

Sucking in a breath, she mumbled, "Thank goodness *that's* over."

HALLIE WOKE with a start and grabbed her phone. "Hello…" she mumbled groggily.

Nobody answered.

Bang! Bang! Bang!

"Let me in!" came a masculine shout.

The jarring command cleared her brain of sleep fog, and she realized the phone hadn't wakened her. Somebody was trying to crash through her apartment door. The bedside clock told her it was three in the morning. Nobody with friendly intentions burst through solid wood to get to you at three in the morning.

She vaulted out of bed and scrambled to find a weapon in the darkness. The lamp! She was about to grab it when—

Bang! Bang! Bang!

"Hallie! Wake up!"

That wasn't the voice of a deranged serial killer. It was Nate! Panic slashed through her as visions of a sick little Trisha burst into her brain. For one fleeting instant she thought she should grab her robe. But concern for the baby overrode her modesty. Deciding her flannel nightgown was perfectly fine, considering a baby's life was at stake, she ran, barefoot, to the door and threw it wide.

"What's the matter?" she shouted over Trisha's gasping wails. The poor baby sounded as if she'd left ordinary pain far behind and was now suffering the tortures of the good and truly damned.

"I need biscotti, and I need it *now,*" Nate yelled. He held his daughter against his shoulder, patting her back. His features were drawn and he looked exhausted. He barged past her and paced the room like a stalking leopard. "She's been crying like this since midnight," he shouted. "Tell me you have biscotti."

Trisha was only having a teething fit. Hallie put a hand over her pounding heart and willed herself to calm down. "My Lord," Hallie cried, "I thought she was bleeding from an artery or at the very least she'd swallowed a nail!"

Nate pivoted and began to stalk in her direction. "I had no idea getting teeth was so damn painful," he growled, and she had a feeling he hadn't heard anything she'd said. His blue eyes were bloodshot, distress was carved on his handsome features. She felt a surge of pity for him. Poor guy. He was trying. She had to give him credit for that. ''You've used up the whole box, already?'' she asked incredulously.

He gritted his teeth and glowered in her direction. ''If you don't have any left, give me the damn recipe.''

His hair was mussed and he looked unforgivably sexy, wearing only those dratted sweatpants. However, this was no time to get on his case about appropriate attire for late-night teething emergencies. ''I don't have any more, Nate.'' She stepped into his path to block his way. ''Will you hold still for a second?''

He almost stumbled into her, but managed to stop in time. She took the baby from his arms. Little Trisha's face was bright red and she was crying as though she thought being cuddled to a broad, perfectly contoured male chest was cruel abuse. Of course, she was young, yet.

''What are we going to do?'' Nate demanded, rubbing his eyes.

Hallie winced at the word ''we,'' but knew she couldn't throw him and his suffering baby out. She carried Trisha to the mauve vinyl sofa and sat. Rubbing a finger along the baby's lower gums, she glanced at Nate. What she was about to suggest already left a bad taste in her mouth. ''I—I guess we could make some.''

Nate's worried expression eased slightly. ''You'd help me?''

Trisha's sobs began to subside, and she grasped Hallie's finger, gumming it frantically. ''I have all the makings,'' she admitted. A thought occurred to her.

"Wait!" She indicated her kitchen with a nod. "I tossed a few broken ones into the cookie jar. That should keep her occupied for a while."

She hadn't finished talking before Nate disappeared into her kitchen. She'd just begun to inhale when he reappeared. He held a chipped biscotti in his raised hand and wore a breath-catching grin on his face. "I never imagined I'd utter these words," he said, "but thank heaven for chocolate biscotti."

Trisha grabbed the cookie from her daddy's fingers and began to gnaw, making sniffling sounds. Tears stopped trailing down her cheeks and her face lost its cherry-red flush. Though the cookie seemed to be working another miracle, Hallie sighed and shook her head. "I hope we don't turn this child into a chocoholic."

"If that happens, I'll take her to the meetings, but right now that's not my biggest problem."

His voice was hoarse with fatigue, and Hallie found that strangely entertaining—Mr. Big Strong Stud, brought to his emotional knees by a pint-size female with only the bare beginnings of teeth. Hallie would bet the farm this guy didn't let a woman get the better of him very often, if ever. She stood, smirking. "You're a little cranky when you haven't had your beauty sleep."

He stared at her, disparagingly, his eyelids at half-mast. "You have a twisted sense of humor, sweetheart. I don't see how anybody could find this funny."

"I don't—not really." She straightened her face, or at least she tried. "Well...not *that* funny." She handed Trisha to her father and picked up a cotton throw that had been folded on the sofa arm. Spreading it over the vinyl, she stepped back so Nate could lay the baby down.

While he did, she dragged a dining room chair up against the sofa seat to keep the baby from rolling off. "Okay, Daddy." She took his arm and tugged him toward the kitchen. "Let's get to work."

When the cookies were finally in the oven, Hallie began to gather dirty dishes and utensils. She picked up the mixing bowl, then put it back down. With a wooden spoon she took a swipe at the chocolate batter clinging to the sides. Holding it toward Nate, she asked, "Want a lick?"

He blinked. The utensil was so close to his face it bumped his nose, leaving a chocolate streak.

"Oops." Hallie laughed. "Sorry. Can you reach it with your tongue?"

He slanted her a quizzical frown. "How long do you think my tongue is?"

She licked the batter off the spoon, grinning at him. Mussed, shirtless, and smeared with chocolate, he looked cute enough to kiss—if she were so inclined to kiss Me-Tarzan types. "Oh," she teased, "you're one of those short-tongued men, huh?"

His gaze narrowed, and she giggled. She was tired. It was now nearly four in the morning and she hadn't slept well even before he'd banged on her door. When she didn't get her full eight hours, sometimes she got a little slaphappy.

Nate rubbed the batter off his nose with the back of his hand. "Short-tongued men?"

She scraped chocolate dough out of the bowl and held the spoon toward him. "Want some more?"

He eyed the spoon for a second before grasping her hand, holding it in his. He took the spoon into his mouth. When he was through, he didn't let go, but guided her hand to lower the spoon into the bowl again. He scraped, then held the spoon to her face. When she opened her mouth, he shifted his hand, brushing the batter along her cheek. "Oops. Better get that with your tongue." He grinned, taunting, "Or are you one of those short-tongued women?"

Eyeing him with pretend vexation, she stuck her tongue out the side of her mouth and found to her regret that she could get nowhere near the batter.

"Need help?"

She lifted her chin. "I could reach it if I wanted, but I like it there." Jerking the spoon from his hold, she scraped at the batter, and with a lightning-quick flourish sent the bowl of the spoon across his chin. "Lick that, Señor Skimpy Tongue!"

He drew back in surprise, his lips quirking. "Don't slander my tongue again, sweetheart! Or it'll cost you."

She scraped at the bowl. "Big talk from Tiny Tongue." She giggled, unable to fathom what was wrong with her. There shouldn't be intoxicating fumes coming from the biscotti batter that would make her act like a lusty drunk.

Unfortunately, Nate's aftershave was making itself known. Maybe he bought that expensive kind with sex pheromones in it. She wouldn't put it past him. And what was worse, it was wearing her out trying to avoid looking at his chest.

Every so often, in the process of moving around in her small kitchen, she had run smack into him—into that warm, hard chest—a graphic reminder that she'd been without a steady boyfriend for a long time. Hallie feared the combination of fatigue and sexual frus-

tration, along with the all-too-near presence of one of
Nature's prime male beef cuts, was causing her to go
a little loony.

"Give me that spoon." He got it without much
effort. When she turned to run, he grabbed her arm.
"You're paying for that Tiny Tongue remark."

She jerked on his hold as he scraped batter. "Don't
you dare," she cried, laughing. "I'll punish you!"

"How?" he asked.

She laughed, enjoying the game and not caring to
analyze why. "I'll—I'll…"

He glazed batter across her lower lip, stopping her
cold. Her laughter dying, Hallie sensed something
about their playfulness had changed.

For several heartbeats he eyed her lips, all kidding
gone from his expression. "Do you want to lick that,
or would you like me to?"

4

HALLIE STARED into Nate's laughing blue eyes, transfixed. Had he taken her kidding around as a sexual overture? What nerve! The thought had never entered her head!

Had it?

Besides, he'd called her bossy. He'd made it perfectly clear that he didn't form relationships with bossy females. But considering the look in his eyes, he didn't have any objection to a quickie with one. Gathering her wits, she pressed against his chest. The palm of her hand tingled at the contact with hard muscle and springy hair. "Uh...you...I mean...do you hear something?"

"No." His grin grew crooked, shrewd. He could tell his toying with her made her nervous. The bum enjoyed knowing he had that power.

"I definitely hear something," she lied, ducking out of range and scurrying toward the living room. Scraping cookie dough from her lower lip with her teeth, she ran to check on Trisha, though she hadn't really heard a thing. As she expected, the baby was sound asleep, the biscotti clutched in her tiny fist, hardly touched.

The sweet darling had exhausted herself and would probably sleep through the rest of the night—not that there was much night left. Lifting a corner of the throw, she covered the baby before hurrying to her bathroom to take a cold washcloth to her face. She not only wanted to wash away the dough, but to get her brain back on track.

She was tired. She needed to slap enough sense into herself to avoid playing games with Nate that included touching. He might not be her type, but he had a lot going for him in the raw sexuality category. Evidently, when she was worn-out, she was more susceptible to making huge mistakes when it came to men. "Don't do anything stupid, Hallie," she muttered, splashing cold water on her face. "You want a man *you* can control, and Nate Hawksmoor isn't even in the same galaxy!"

REFRESHED after sleeping until ten, Hallie puttered around her apartment and did a little bookkeeping work to get ahead. In the afternoon, she did some grocery shopping, relieved that Nate was leaving her alone. She'd expected to see him at her door first thing that morning with another teething emergency or a diaper crisis or something. But by the time she'd left her apartment an hour ago, she had neither heard from him nor seen him.

She only hoped he hadn't called on Buffy for assistance. He could do better calling a turnip! As she climbed the steps to her second-floor apartment, she frowned at herself. "Hallie, get off it!" she mumbled. "That baby is not your business, and whether Nate calls Buffy or not is even less your concern!"

As she shifted her groceries to retrieve her key, she thought she heard something. Experiencing a surge of unease, she turned to look at Nate's door. Was Trisha crying? She took a couple of steps toward his door, then stopped, straining to hear. Oh, dear. There was definite wailing going on in there. She sighed, torn. She knew she should turn away, take her groceries into her apartment and leave Nate to his own problems. She didn't want to get her heart tangled up with his baby. But even as she counseled herself to stay out of it, she was testing his doorknob to see if it was locked.

The knob turned and the latch lifted. Against her better judgment she went inside. There was nobody in the living room. Walking farther in, she called out. "Nate?"

No answer. Evidently the baby's sobs were drowning out her voice. She could tell the crying came from the kitchen, and she pictured Nate trying to calm another of Trisha's teething fits with one of their late-night-baked biscotti. Hurrying toward the sound, she lay her grocery sacks on his dining room table and swung into the kitchen.

What she saw made her skid to a stop. Nate held Trisha by her hands, aloft over the sink, washing her squirmy body with a soapy washcloth.

Letting out a horrified gasp, she rushed over and rescued the howling baby, cuddling her to her breast. "Are you nuts?" she cried. "You're not plucking a chicken here. This is a baby!"

Nate's initial look of surprise turned to a frown. "Good Lord, woman, don't sneak up on people."

"I didn't sneak up on you!" She rocked the baby gently in her arms, trying to calm her. "Trisha was screaming so loud, you didn't hear me."

His frown didn't ease, but something came into his eyes that looked like doubt. "I was giving her a bath."

"You don't dangle a child over the sink to bathe her. That's how you clean muddy boots!" Grabbing the towel Nate had laid out, she wrapped up the child to keep her from getting chilled.

He leaned a hip against the counter and looked down at the floor. After a few seconds he passed her a sidelong glance. "Hell. Did I hurt her?"

Hallie felt an unwanted rush of compassion. She shook her head. "No." With great regret, she added, "I'll show you how to bathe a baby. And I'll help you with her for the rest of this week." She met his gaze, her attitude uncompromising. "But after the holidays, you hire a nanny!" She was miffed at herself for getting involved with Nate's daughter, after she'd vowed she'd never, *ever,* let herself be vulnerable to the pain of separation again. But how could any right-thinking person refuse to help after seeing how laughably inept Nate was at caring for his baby? If anything happened to Trisha, Hallie could never forgive herself.

"I won't say I don't need your help." His expression was less thrilled than she would have thought. "Thanks."

"You're welcome." She felt a foolish charge of excitement, and glanced at Trisha. The baby had stopped crying and was looking up at her with those big, inquisitive eyes. She smiled at the baby. "Don't panic, sweetie, but we're going to try that bath again. Then you, Daddy and I are going shopping in *my* car. And the first thing we're buying the old man is an instruction book on how not to kill you."

HALLIE DECIDED that if she was going to cook dinner again for the two of them, she'd rather do it in her own kitchen. At seven-thirty, dinner was over and the dishes done. Hallie and Nate settled in her living room to go through the baby care reference book she'd insisted he purchase. The book was only one small item out of several hundred dollars' worth of baby merchandise they'd bought. Nate made it through the afternoon, but he was marginally shell-shocked from how much babies cost to care for, clothe and feed.

Now, Trisha slept peacefully beside Hallie, the teething remedy they'd bought making life more bearable for everybody. Nate sat very near Hallie's other side, his thigh pressed against hers. Unfortunately, there was no getting around his nearness. They couldn't pore over the same book and still maintain their distance.

He smelled nice, but she tried not to notice. That was getting to be a habit with her—trying not to notice attractive things about Nate Hawksmoor. He'd been pretty darned cute with the baby that afternoon. It had been impossible not to notice. There was something special about watching a man with his baby daughter.

That special something hadn't gone unnoticed by salesgirls at the baby stores, either. Young mothers lugging squalling infants had been totally ignored while Nate got brisk service from every fluttery, eyelash-flapping female employee in the stores. Even female managers came flocking out of back offices.

Once, Hallie had actually been elbowed into a display of Dipi Wipies. She had been forced to pick herself up and restack the boxes while the salesclerks hovered around Nate, oblivious to anything else. If the whole spectacle hadn't been so revolting, it might have been funny.

"Babies get cholera?" Nate asked, breaking through her thoughts.

She frowned, rereading the sentence. "Colic," she corrected.

"What's that?"

"Basically, a stomachache. The book tells you what to do." She turned the page. "See, here's a—"

A noise drew Hallie's attention—the rattling of a key in her front door.

"What the hell?" Nate reacted by standing up. Obviously his Me-Tarzan, macho personality was preparing for a confrontation.

"It's okay." Hallie touched his hand. "It's—"

The door swung open and a tall, good-looking cowboy exploded into the apartment. All smiles, clad in a flannel shirt, down vest, jeans and black Stetson, he stumbled to a halt. His grin faded slightly. Moss-green eyes roved over the domestic scene. "I know I've been gone awhile, darlin'," he said, "but I didn't know I'd been gone *that* long!"

Hallie smiled and stood, hurrying to give him a hug. "Sugar!" she cried. "This is a nice surprise. Merry Christmas."

"Merry Christmas yourself, darlin'," he drawled. "I brought you somethin'."

Hallie stepped out of his embrace as he turned around to grab up his duffel and a brightly-wrapped package. She held on to her smile, but winced inwardly. Sugar was a sweet, thoughtful friend and ex-lover, but on a scale of one to ten, where ten was megatacky, Sugar's gifts rated a forty.

"Oh, Sugar, you shouldn't have."

He handed her a box about the size of a six-pack. "Heck, not get you somethin' when I come through T-Town? What do you think I am, a tightwad toady?"

"Of course not." She accepted the gift with resigned sufferance, and kissed his cheek. "Come on in."

The sound of a throat being cleared drew her attention and she glanced toward Nate. He was watching Sugar with a jaundiced eye. Taking the cowboy's hand, she tugged him to the couch. "Sugar, this is Nate Hawksmoor, my landlord, from across the hall. And this is his baby, Trisha." Deciding Sugar didn't need the details, she added, "He just got custody of the baby, and I'm helping him get things he needs."

Sugar held out a big, square paw. "Good to meet you, ol' buddy."

Nate shook Sugar's hand. "Likewise," he said, though he didn't smile. Letting go, he asked, "Mind if I don't call you Sugar?"

Sugar laughed, and Trisha jumped in her sleep. The cowboy's laughter tended toward furniture-rattling guffaws. Hallie held up a quieting finger and nodded toward the baby.

Sugar made an apologetic face and squinted at Nate, whispering, "The name's Sugarbush. Wayne Sugarbush, ol' buddy." He winked. "Everybody calls me Sugar. It's my handle. Well, actually, Sugar Burger."

"Classy," Nate muttered.

Hallie gave Nate a warning look. Though Sugar didn't tend to pick up on sarcasm, she did. His glance only met hers for an instant before he went on. "I gather you're a trucker, Wayne?"

"Yep." Sugar swept off his Stetson and sailed it toward the dining area where it landed soundlessly in the center of the chrome-and-glass table.

Hallie watched Nate's gaze follow the hat's flight path. Tiny frown lines formed between his eyes. She wondered what was wrong, then decided he was probably ticked because his private tutoring session had been interrupted. "When I hit Tulsa," Sugar went on, "I always stop for a visit with Hallie." He hugged her hard. "I wouldn't shove on through town without seeing my best gal."

She smiled through the pain of his hug. Sugar was a big puppy dog of a man. But even as big and strong as he was, when they'd been a couple he'd been completely controllable, amenable to her every whim. But no matter how slavish he might be, inside that good-looking husk, Sugar was a kid who would never grow up.

She loved him like a brother now and, true to form, Sugar was just fine with that. She wished she could love him differently; he was perfect for her needs. But he didn't stimulate her mind. After a few months of being Sugar's "boss lady," as he'd liked to call her, she was so bored she wanted to scream.

Consequently she'd insisted their relationship become platonic. That had been a week before she'd moved into this apartment. These days, when Sugar came through town and dropped by, he crashed on her couch, never failing to bring something well-meant but tacky.

"Aren't you going to open your gift?" Sugar asked, scarily on cue.

"Oh—sure." She took her place on the sofa and

lay the package on the glass surface of the coffee table.

She could feel Nate sit back. Sugar dropped down to sit cross-legged on the carpet on the other side of the coffee table.

Once Hallie had the brown corrugated box out of the wrappings, she opened it to find a stuffed toy. A fuzzy white buffalo. It was smoking a pipe. "Oh…why…my goodness," she said, truly in awe. This was *amazingly* tacky. Maybe not as tacky as the paperweight with a real tarantula imbedded in plastic, but close. "I don't know what to say."

Sugar flicked the toy with a finger. "Would you believe that little darlin' only cost me thirty-two bucks?"

"I can't believe it," Nate murmured, and Hallie cast him a quelling look. He shrugged, a thoroughly unrepentant twinkle in his eyes.

"I was knocked on my ass to find they'd put that little guy on sale." Sugar shook his head and chuckled. "Some people can't see what's first class and what's not."

"How true," Nate said, his voice edged with mirth. "I gather you gave Hallie all that framed fake money hanging on her kitchen wall?"

Sugar grinned. "Yep. My favorite is J. Edgar on that thirteen-dollar bill. Get it? I figure it's because—"

"I get it." Nate picked up the baby book and stood. He faced Hallie. "Thanks for the help today." He held out a hand. "Good night."

Hallie had been the one to leave abruptly the night before, and he'd been startled. Now it was her turn.

She glanced at his outstretched hand with reservations. She'd held this man's hand once, and had decided to avoid making that mistake again. Nodding, she shifted to pick up Trisha.

"Don't bother," he said. "I'll get her."

"It was great to meet you, Nate, ol' buddy." Sugar rose from the carpet.

"Right." Nate gently lifted his sleeping daughter into his arms. "Merry Christmas." He glanced at Hallie. "And thanks again."

She walked to the door with him, opening it. She felt an odd sense of abandonment, or loss, or something. A ridiculous feeling. She shook it off. "Look, if you need anything else or have any more questions…"

He glanced her way. "Sure." His gaze traveled to Sugar and then back to her. Just as he had taken his first step out the door, he stopped and turned back. "Say, Wayne, we were trying to figure out who Dr. Spock is. Do you know?"

Sugar scratched his chin, his brow knitting. "Isn't he that guy on 'Star Trek'?"

"With the pointy ears?" Nate suggested helpfully.

Snapping his fingers, Sugar beamed. "Yep. That's the guy."

Nate passed Hallie a meaninfgul look, his lips quirking. "Fascinating," he murmured.

By the time Hallie closed the door, she was fuming. Drat the man. What did he think he proved with *that* remark?

IT SURPRISED NATE to discover that it bothered him to leave Hallie alone with that good-natured, tacky-gift-buying moose. Somehow he didn't picture her as the casual sex type. She certainly hadn't given off any

"I'm available" vibes to him. Well, maybe that one biscotti thing in the middle of the night. But they'd both been bushed. She wasn't thinking right when she'd smeared him with batter, and his brain cells had been misfiring pretty badly by the time he'd had that insane urge to kiss her. He credited both lapses to nervous exhaustion.

Even so, he'd avoided asking for her help all day, and he would have gone on avoiding her if she hadn't barged in on him. She was domineering and over-bearing and, after seeing Sugar, it was hilariously clear that she was determined to be the head honcho in her relationships with men.

No way was he getting hot and bothered over that woman.

No damn way!

NATE WAS UP EARLY Sunday morning, thanks to Trisha's assumption that if she didn't eat every four hours she would die of starvation. He fed her with slightly more success than a basset hound might have had doing the same thing. After cleaning up, he settled his daughter on a blanket in front of the fireplace.

Nate enjoyed lounging on the rug, reading the Sunday paper before a blazing fire. Unfortunately, few days in Oklahoma were cold enough to merit a fire. And even fewer of those days came on Sundays.

He'd given his staff the week off, but he wasn't quite as lucky. He had one appointment this afternoon that he hadn't been able to avoid. Otherwise, this week was a vacation he badly needed. He hadn't expected to spend it quite this way, however.

Trisha made a cooing sound and he glanced at her. She seemed to be examining her fingers as if she'd never seen them before. He smiled and patted her cheek. "I'll get the paper and read you the funnies. And when I'm an old codger without any teeth, you can feed me my cereal and read the sports section to me. How's that, kid?"

Big baby eyes blinked, staring at him. She held a hand toward him, wagging her fingers.

"I'll take that as a definite yes." Bounding up, he went to his apartment door and opened it just as the door across the hall swung wide. He felt a twinge of disquiet to see the fullback-size cowboy standing there—in baggy red shorts and nothing else. His brawny, muscled chest was coated with thick, black fur. Sugar caught sight of Nate and grinned. "Morning, ol' buddy." Scratching his hip, he squatted to get the paper.

"Morning." Nate surveyed Hallie's visitor with a squint of disapproval. He looked a little too peppy for six-thirty in the morning. Nate felt as if nails had been driven into his eyeballs and knew he looked like a character out of *The Attack of the Red-Eyed Zombies.*

Rising with a yawn, Sugar slapped the paper against one strapping, hairy leg. "Sleep well?"

Nate nodded and grinned thinly. "Like a top."

Sugar guffawed. "Buddy, I never understood that old saying. Seems like it'd mean you spun around all night."

"Yeah, well…" The guy was probably closer to the truth than he knew. "And you?" Nate gritted his teeth. Why had he asked that? He didn't need details.

"Me?" Sugar's laugh rang in the hallway and he swatted the newspaper against his leg a couple more times. "You know Hallie."

What the hell did that mean? With a lame chuckle,

Nate nodded. "Yeah, well…" He lifted his paper as if to suggest that he held in his hand news stories in urgent need of reading. "See ya—old buddy." Ducking inside his apartment, Nate wondered why the friendly, hairy baboon irritated the hell out of him.

Nate would have sworn three days had crawled by since he'd seen Sugar getting Hallie's newspaper. Had it really only been six hours? Six hours, eight diaper changes, two meals, a semi-successful bath for Trisha and a shower for him—during which he'd come dangerously close to falling asleep.

At half-past noon, he tried to eat a sandwich while feeding Trisha messy, slobbery bites of cereal. The bib Hallie had insisted he buy had been a good idea. It sported a plastic pocket that went all the way across the bottom, catching food Trisha spit out.

He thought he was getting the hang of feeding her. He'd begun to master the art of using the cereal spoon as if he was shaving her, catching cereal as it dribbled down her chin. He'd then scrape the retrieved cereal back into her mouth. There wasn't nearly as much food falling into the bib pocket as there had been at breakfasts number one or two. And the baby carrier Hallie had insisted he get propped Trisha at exactly the right angle for feeding, which also made life easier. He had to give Hallie points. She'd saved his bacon these past two days.

"Go ahead and spit it out, Tee," he challenged, lowering his face to within an inch of hers. "Make my day."

Trisha gurgled and bubbled and opened her mouth. When she did, Nate slid the spoon inside. "Ha! Gotcha!"

Trisha flapped her arms like an awkward bird and spewed out the bite, obviously enjoying the game.

"Young ladies do not slobber food down their chins," he stated with a wry chuckle. "Daddy does *not* think that's funny. He is *not* laughing."

She sputtered with glee, grabbing his nose with a sticky hand.

"Tee!" He sat back, eyeing her with grudging amusement. "New rule. Grabbing the schnozzola means lunch is over."

She gurgled, clapping her hands together.

"Oh, yeah? Well, I'm glad it's over, too, sweetcakes. Besides, we have to get going."

He didn't like the idea of taking her along to Grand Lake. But he'd made the appointment two weeks ago. This was the only time his clients could meet with him on their lakefront lot to go over architectural plans for their retirement home.

He especially didn't relish the idea of strapping Trisha into his two-seater, considering what Hallie had said about air bags. But he had little choice at the moment.

As he cleaned her up, he frowned. Worried. He was dead on his feet, but he couldn't impose on Hallie again. Especially not when she had her big lug of a lover visiting. "Hell," he muttered, walking into the living room to shift Trisha from her carrier into the portable car seat. "I'll stop for coffee every fifteen minutes, huh, Tee?"

She lifted her arms, wiggling fingers at him.

"You can cry if you want. Real loud."

Her eyelids dipped and she made a cooing sound. Her eyes closed.

"Oh, fine," he whispered. "*Now* you sleep."

A knock on his door brought his head up with a jerk. When he opened it he was startled to see Hallie there, clad in a lavender mock-turtle sweater and formfitting jeans. Her hair shone. She had on a touch of lipstick and she smelled nice. She also looked damn fine, as if she'd had a relaxing bubble bath or good sex or something. "Hi," he said, puzzled.

She smiled at him. "Everything okay?"

He shrugged. "Fine."

She peered past him, as though she wanted to come in to check for herself. "Trisha?"

Disgruntled that she didn't give him any credit for being able to care for an infant, he stepped aside so she could see the baby on the sofa. "She's not dead. Just asleep."

Hallie glanced at him, then back at the car seat. "She's sleeping in that?" She tiptoed past him to get a closer look.

"We're leaving for the afternoon."

She turned to frown at him. "Leaving?"

"I'm meeting a client at Grand Lake in an hour and a half."

"And you're taking the baby? In *your* car?"

He experienced a stab of exasperation. She might look cute, but she was still a bully. "No, I thought we'd hitchhike," he muttered. "Don't you have company?"

She spotted the tote bag sitting next to the couch and bent to unzip it. "Sugar needed to be in Corpus Christi by tonight, so he left after breakfast." She began to dig around inside the bag.

He didn't know how he felt about her overnighter with the grinning, hulking cowboy, but knew that feeling anything but total disinterest was a bad idea. "What are you doing?"

"Checking to make sure you have everything she'll need. And just as I thought, you don't."

"Yes, I do," he said, making no effort to mask his annoyance.

She straightened. "You should always pack for twice as long as you think you'll be gone. Just in case of an emergency."

He ground his teeth. "Look, I appreciate your help, but that doesn't give you any blasted right to say I'm wrong."

Clearly taken aback by his outburst, she lifted her chin. "Forgive me," she said calmly. "What word is it your girlfriends say to let you know you're—incorrect?"

Hellfire! The woman could be maddening! He knew he shouldn't have blown. Obviously he was too exhausted to think straight. In truth, he was more angry with himself than with her. The smooth setup Ol' Smiles-Like-A-Satisfied-Ape Sugar had with her filled him with idiotic resentment, and that annoyed him to no end. Eyeing her grimly, he opened his mouth to apologize.

"My father never liked to be told he was wrong, either," she cut in. "He's screwing up his third marriage right now. Men like you make me barf." Spinning away, she marched into his bedroom.

He changed his mind about apologizing, but made an effort to rein in his temper. A minute later she came out with diapers and several cans of formula. Stuffing them into the bag, she glanced at him. "You look terrible, by the way."

He crossed his arms over his chest, squelching an

urge to strangle her. "I hear it's chic to look half dead."

She eyed him with skepticism for a long minute. Casting her glance away, she seemed to be wrestling with some deep, dark problem. Maybe she wanted to strangle him, too, and was weighing her odds. "I tell you what," she finally said, looking serious, almost resigned. "We'll use my car. My front passenger seat reclines. I'll drive. You sleep."

He was more than surprised. An offer to drive was at the other end of the spectrum from strangulation. He knew her suggestion was made out of pity, and he didn't relish the fact one bit. "I don't think so."

"Don't be stupid, Nate. You'll fall asleep at the wheel and kill yourself and Trisha. Is your macho pride worth all that?"

He eyed her with umbrage. The only thing he hated more than a woman's pity was to have her telling him what to do. Unfortunately he was too beat to do much more than blink. He had to meet his client today. Hallie was right. His choices ranged all the way from few to none.

"Then it's settled." She grabbed the tote bag and brushed by him. "You get Trisha and I'll fetch my keys."

He watched Hallie disappear into her apartment before slouching against his doorjamb. "Damn it, woman," he growled.

A long, soul-searching moment came and went while his dubious gaze remained fixed on her door.

"Thanks," he muttered, the word tainted with irony.

5

HALLIE WAS WILLING to go on record that she had completely lost her mind. What had possessed her to venture across the hall this afternoon? Her knuckles whitened on the steering wheel of her Taurus sedan as she let herself think about her stupidity. Glancing in her rearview mirror, she could see little Trisha sleeping like an angel, her head lolled to the side. She was so young, so innocent, so hard to resist.

Casting a reluctant glance toward Nate, she felt a painful tug somewhere in her midsection. He looked like an angel, too—when he was asleep—a darned cute masculine one. On second thought, he was too sexy for any entity that might sport a halo and wings. And unlike his baby daughter, Nate was hardly innocent. She hoped fervently he was easier to resist. *Memo to me,* she cautioned herself. *Avoid him when he's sleeping.*

He'd dozed off moments after they'd left the apartment complex, which was just as well. Their quibbling would have disturbed Trisha.

She cast him another sidelong look and scowled. There was nothing worse than a good-looking, pain-in-the-neck, domineering man!

He moved, shifting toward her. With a deep breath, he opened his lips slightly, as though preparing for a kiss. Her heart did a little pirouette and she swallowed hard. Jerking her gaze back to the road, she clamped her jaws together. So what if he had Val Kilmer lips, or were they Tom Cruise lips? Maybe she should take another peek to make absolutely—

Hallie, get your mouth off his lips—I mean your mind—get your mind off his lips and drive the car!

She had an impulse to cough really loudly to wake him up. In such close quarters, it was better to fight with the guy than to conjure up weird fantasies that would take her nowhere but into the kind of trouble her mother had suffered with her father. *No thank you, Mr. Hawksmoor.*

She reached for her window crank. Fresh air would dilute the scent of the man beside her. She stopped. The weak winter sun had slunk away to cower behind ashen clouds and the weather was growing colder by the minute. Trisha didn't need a frigid wind blowing in her face just so Hallie could rid herself of troubling Nate-tinged air.

The day had grown bleak. Bleak and gray, like her mood. Unhappily, the worst of it was, she had nobody to blame for her predicament but her stupid, buttinsky self.

HALLIE SAT IN THE BACK seat of her car. Nate had directed her to park on a hill overlooking Grand Lake, nestled in the rolling hills of eastern Oklahoma. Trisha had awakened as soon as they'd pulled to a stop, so Hallie had moved back there to cuddle her. Turning Trisha in her arms so the baby could look out the window, she said, "See Daddy?" Nate and the couple for whom he was building the retirement home were strolling through the lovely treed lot, which overlooked the choppy lake.

Nate looked very *GQ* in a chestnut-brown wool overcoat and matching leather gloves. Tassel loafers topped off his preppy facade. She supposed doing business with wealthy retirees, he needed to make a certain impression. He had to look like a confident, ultraconservative wearer of natural fibers. Nate gestured broadly toward the water while speaking to the couple. Both the husband and wife seemed petite next to Nate. They appeared affluent, dressed impeccably—also in natural fibers.

Nate grinned and said something, causing the couple to laugh. A gust of wind fluttered his thick hair. From her vantage point, Hallie could see his profile. A wisp of dark coffee-colored hair tumbled across his forehead; he gestured again, brushing it back. The movement was smooth and strangely sensual.

She found herself enjoying the sight of him. He exuded success, competence, and one-hundred-percent scrumptiousness. He put an arm around the older man's shoulders. The man nodded as Nate offered his wife an arm. Guiding them toward the water, he spoke. Both clients smiled.

"He's a charmer, your daddy," Hallie murmured, startled to hear her thought voiced out loud. She bent to look at Trisha. The wide-eyed infant stared out the window, her tongue playing tag with her fingers. Hallie had a feeling Trisha wasn't paying strict attention to her handsome father. "Listen, Trisha," she whispered. "If it's all the same to you, I wouldn't repeat my last remark. Okay?"

Trisha sputtered.

"Good. Thanks." Hallie sat up in time to see Nate wave to the couple as they headed toward their luxury car. Hurriedly, Hallie secured Trisha in her car seat and opened the door. The cold air hit her so hard it made her gasp. The temperature had dropped past freezing, and the windchill made matters worse. She scrambled into the driver's seat. When Nate got in on the passenger's side, he leaned back and closed his eyes. "I hope I made sense," he said through a tired groan.

Hallie experienced a pang of sympathy. That hour's nap he'd had on the way up hadn't been enough sleep. "You looked like you were making sense to me."

He glanced her way. "The cold air helped." His grin did something weird to her insides.

"So, what was in the tube you gave them?"

"The preliminary drawings. Now they'll go home and decide what they want changed. Usually that requires routing water pipes through the kitchen table or putting a picture window behind the refrigerator." He chuckled and closed his eyes, sinking back against the seat. "But eventually we'll get it worked out so it can actually be built."

She smiled. She knew how it was to work with people. And in a creative field like architecture, it had to get crazy from time to time. "Have you built any other houses on Grand Lake?"

He didn't open his eyes. "Half dozen or so."

"Really?" Curious about this creative side of the man, she couldn't help but ask, "Can we drive by one or two? I'd love to see them."

He opened one eye, squinting at her. "Why?"

She was amused by his suspicious attitude. "I'll try to resist saying you designed them wrong."

He opened the other eye, his expression doubtful.

She laughed. "Okay, okay, I absolutely promise!" She flashed a three-finger pledge. "Scout's honor. No matter how excruciating it is to keep my mouth shut, I won't say a word.''

His lips twisted in a crooked grin. "Okay, sweetheart. If you promise to suffer, I'm in.''

She started the car. "Which way?''

They drove by several homes that Nate had designed for the parklike tracts that hugged Grand Lake. No matter how hard Hallie tried, she wasn't even close to suffering. His architectural style was pleasing to the senses, his houses unencumbered by complicated facades. Each residence, in its own unique way, exhibited a great deal of attention to openness and natural light.

As they drove, it started spitting snow. Not enough to be worrisome. On the contrary, it was rather pretty, sprinkling down over the quiet wooded countryside.

When Nate pointed out his most recently completed home, Hallie pulled to a stop on the blacktop lane. She could only gape. A meticulously landscaped path meandered lazily through trees to a secluded residence constructed of stone, glass, and dark-stained timber. Sheltered on all sides by lofty native oak and pines, the quietly elegant structure seemed to fit into the scenery as though it had grown from it.

"Why did you stop?'' Nate asked.

She blinked, coming out of her trance. Shaking herself, she adjusted her expression before she faced him. "Hmm?''

He lay an arm across the back of her seat and leaned toward her. "I said, why did you stop?'' His smile was quizzical.

She turned away, bothered by her pulse-pounding reaction.

"Suffering?'' he taunted.

The smug bum. He knew she was impressed. She smirked, facing him. "I'm in agony."

He cocked his head, looking skeptical and maybe a little hurt.

"Okay, okay!" she admitted. "They're gorgeous. If I could afford you, I'd hire you right now."

"Thanks." This time the grin he flashed had the effect of a stun gun. "If you could afford me, I'd let you."

"Aren't you democratic," she teased.

He nodded toward the windshield. "Drive. I'll show you my lot."

She stared at him, startled. "You have a lot here?" The question came out in a whisper.

"A client owned two, so he paid me with one of them for drawing up plans for his lake place and his residence in south Tulsa."

After rounding a curve, he pointed. "There."

She pulled to a stop and sat back to take in their surroundings. The snow fell steadily now. Big, fluffy flakes were glazing Nate's land, which was located on a rise dotted with big trees. All but the pines and oaks were winter-bare, stark but beautiful against the pewter sky. Even from the road Hallie could see a vast expanse of the lake stretching out in front of them. "Well…" she murmured, unable to think of anything worthy to say.

"Doesn't exactly suck," he said.

She laughed at his comical lack of swagger, her attitude about him inching up a notch. "Absolute minimal sucking." Taking her foot off the brake, she started forward, driving slowly so she could scan the tract and its view. "So, when are you building your dream home?"

"When I can afford one."

She grinned, peeking his way. His eyes glinted with a pleasant, teasing light. Her heart stumbled, then settled back into rhythm. "I guess we'd better be heading back, huh?" For some reason the question held a wistful note.

"I'm not sure we should," he said. "Your tires are on the bald side. We might as well have dinner and wait out the storm. It's not supposed to do much."

She was starving, having skipped lunch. So the idea didn't exactly suck, either. "Okay. Besides, Trisha needs to eat."

Nate glanced over his shoulder at his daughter. Trisha was watching them, but her eyelids were drooping. "Looks like somebody in this car is pretty boring."

Hallie glanced in the rearview mirror. "Somebody in this car is a precious heartbreaker."

"Precious is a bit much, but thanks," Nate said.

She eyed him pointedly. "And there's somebody else in this car—a nonfemale who has an ego that could flatten New York City." She fought to keep from showing amusement. The man was incorrigible and should not be encouraged.

"Turn left onto the main road." His lips quirked, the unrepentant good-for-nothing. "Erma's Place is a couple of miles ahead."

"Who's Erma?" The strange touch of petulance in her question came out of nowhere.

"I'm not sure she exists. Erma's Place is a refurbished farmhouse. The downstairs is a café. The bedrooms upstairs are rented out, like a motel." He took off his gloves and stuffed them into his overcoat pocket. "They serve the best chicken-fried steak I've ever had."

Erma's Place looked exactly like any other white frame farmhouse, except for the sign out front, flashing V can y.

Hallie laughed. "'V can y'?" She pulled into the gravel parking lot. "Makes you wonder if they have a vacancy or if the 'No' is just burned out, too."

"Since there's one other car in the lot, I'd say they have several 'V can y's."

Hallie grinned at him and he grinned back. The brief connection had an odd impact on her. She had to drag her gaze away to turn off the engine.

The café was charmingly folksy and nearly empty when they walked in. But as the snow began to fall in earnest more travelers arrived to wait it out.

Though Hallie ached to fuss over Trisha and feed her, she made herself sit across from father and daughter in their booth, letting Nate get the practice. He held Trisha in his arms, feeding her a bottle.

Several times, couples stopped by their table and goo-gooed at the baby, leaving with overloud whispers of "What a cute family." Hallie was unsettled by the assumption, and she could see by Nate's pinched eyebrows that he was, too. They were not a family, and neither Nate nor Hallie had the slightest interest in becoming one. The light mood they'd shared while sight-seeing was broken, and when their dinners came, they ate in silence.

"It's coming down hard," Nate commented.

Hallie jumped at the sound of his voice. She looked out the window. Even in the dusky light she could see that he was right. It was snowing furiously. She didn't know when she'd seen the like before in Oklahoma.

"It looks like a blizzard," she murmured. She'd only seen one once, on a family vacation in Colorado. Her dad, stepmother, and the girls had been stranded at a truck stop for six hours. It was impossible to see two feet ahead that day. Ever since, she'd had no desire to see another blizzard, ever.

"We might have to stay here tonight." His jaws clenched and she could tell he wasn't any more delighted with the notion than she. "I'll go ask the proprietor if he's heard anything about road conditions or how long the snow might last."

Hallie sipped her coffee. This was a bad turn of events. She hadn't planned for an overnight trip. She cast a gaze at Trisha, sitting on the table in her portable car seat, and tweaked her bootied foot. "At least you've got provisions, sweetie."

Trisha had been eyeing the Christmas decorations strung above the booths. Twinkling lights flashed on and off amid plastic greenery and red bows. When her foot was tweaked, she looked at Hallie. Suddenly her baby features opened in a grin and she gurgled.

Hallie was startled and touched. Even in her dour mood, she smiled back. When a baby smiled, everybody who saw it smiled. It was as much a natural law as gravity or survival of the fittest. Hallie took hold of Trisha's little foot and kissed her toes. "Don't weave your spell around me, young lady," she warned softly. "And a good start would be never doing that to me again. Is that clear?"

Trisha gurgled, her mouth bubbling. She broke into another toothless grin.

"Cruel, cruel baby," Hallie admonished, smiling back.

"We're stuck here."

Hallie jumped and Nate slid into the booth. Her smile fading, she asked, "What do you mean?"

He shrugged, laying several bills on the table. "The forecast is for eight inches. A semitrailer has jack-knifed on the highway, so the road's closed until further notice. I reserved a room."

Hallie experienced a prick of misgiving. "You mean *rooms,* don't you?"

He shook his head, looking serious. "With the weather turning bad, the place was filling up. It was all I could get."

"It?"

The waitress swung by and swept up the money, breezing off before Nate spoke. "I'm sorry. If you want, I can sleep in the car."

"Oh, sure. In a blizzard?" She ran a hand through her bangs. "What would I get for that? Manslaughter?" She slumped against the padding of the plastic booth.

After a moment of strained silence, he asked, "Are you weighing the pros and cons?" His smile was crooked, but more weary than amused.

She crossed her arms in front of her. "One night with you versus ten years in prison?" She let her pause linger.

"Well?"

"I'm thinking," she mumbled, not wholly kidding. She didn't like the idea of being cloistered in a room with this man where there was a chance both of them would end up horizontal. She didn't believe in one-night stands, especially not with a landlord—no matter how good-looking. Besides, Nate might be a talented architect and a gorgeous male specimen, but he wanted submissive women in his life. Hallie didn't fit that mold and had no intention of trying.

"Very funny," he said.

She decided her taunting had gone on long enough. "Look…" She sat forward. "I'm glad you had the foresight to reserve a room. Trisha doesn't need to spend a night in the ditch in a blizzard." She placed her forearms on the table and leaned toward him. "And even though we're not crazy about each other, we're mature adults. We can do this. Pioneers probably did it all the time."

He scanned her face, his expression quizzical. "Pioneers probably did what all the time? Stay in one hotel room?"

She grinned against her will. "I meant, rough it."

"You consider spending the night with me 'roughing it'?"

"I consider spending the night with you off the roughing it scale, Mr. Hawksmoor." She eyed him levelly. "No offense."

He ran a hand across his chin, watching her with those remarkable eyes. He smiled, then. It was a good smile that warmed her insides far more than it should. "No offense taken, Miss St. John."

A strange tremor darted through her, and she couldn't fathom why.

THIS WAS A BAD TIME for Nate to discover he had the hots for Hallie St. John. Snow battered the window in the hotel's upstairs bedroom, a depressing reminder that nobody was going anywhere for a while.

He checked his watch. Seven-thirty. Even as worn-out as he was, it was too early to go to sleep—especially when he'd promised to platonically share the bed with a woman who stimulated him physically like none other in recent memory. Emotionally, on the other hand, they were locked in continuous combat, each attempting to shoot the other down, to become the winner, the *boss*.

But physically...

He yawned, watching her as she pulled back the covers and gently placed Trisha in the middle of the bed, near the headboard. She positioned a pillow on either side of the infant. As Hallie fixed and fluffed, her derriere wiggled and waggled in Nate's direct line of vision.

Did she know what shoving that rounded, feminine morsel of anatomy at his face did to him? *Get a grip, Hawksmoor,* he chided himself.

Ol' Buddy Sugar Burger was her current stud. She wasn't in the market for a man. The words "You know Hallie" echoed in his memory, and visions of wild sex games with his pretty, pushy neighbor filled his brain. Irritation swelled inside him at his mental wanderings. Hallie was as far from his type as...as General Norman Schwarzkopf.

She straightened, and Nate retreated a hasty half step, pretending to examine the Native American print hanging beside the window. *Nate, my friend, make one false move toward that woman and she'll head-butt you out that second-story window. Is that really how you want to die?*

He yawned again and shook his head. It might be seven-thirty, but he could use some shut-eye.

"You're tired," Hallie said.

"Big-time." He glanced at her, his grin rueful and a little guilty, which he hoped she wouldn't detect.

With pinched brows, Hallie glanced around. He knew what she was looking for. Something—anything—for him to sleep on. The room unfortunately was pretty plain. There was one straight-backed chair beside the door, a dresser upon which an old TV perched, a postage-stamp-size bathroom-with-shower, and an indentation in the wall that served as a closet. Woe be it to anybody who traveled with more than one change of clothes.

"I'm too tired to hassle you, if that's what you're afraid of," he said, wishing he meant it. Still and all, if Hallie knew anything about men, she knew they were never *that* tired—unless they were dead.

Men really were pigs, he supposed. Funny, Hallie was the first woman who'd ever made him see that about his gender. Maybe it was because he knew she had no intention of sleeping with him, which was not an experience he'd encountered with women who shared his bedroom. And he had to confess, compatible or not, if Hallie showed any interest, he sure wouldn't kick her out of bed. On the other hand, if she kept giving off "I wouldn't let you touch me if you were the last man on earth" vibes, he could possibly force himself to simply go to sleep.

"What are you going to sleep in?" she asked, looking worried.

He was confused. "I was hoping for a piece of the bed."

She shook her head. "I mean, *wear*. What are you going to wear?"

He grinned, teasing, "What are *you* going to wear?"

Her cheeks turned pink and she cast a despondent glance toward the window. The frilly curtains were tied back to reveal glimpses of snow swirling violently. The windowpanes rattled under the onslaught of the wind. Nate could tell she was willing the storm to disappear. After a moment, when the snow refused to vanish, she returned her unenthusiastic glance to his face. "I'll just take off my jeans and shoes, I guess."

He shrugged out of his sports jacket and hung it in the wall niche beside his overcoat. "For you, I'll leave on my briefs."

She blushed fiercely and turned away. "Well…just turn off the lights before you, uh…"

"Undress?"

She moved to the side of the bed and sat, tugging off her loafers. When she unsnapped her waistband, she glanced his way, her face somber. "And stay on your side of the baby."

Unfastening his belt buckle, he couldn't help grinning. "Now who's got the inflated ego?" Pulling out his belt, he tossed it on the chair. Hallie's back was to him now. She began to wriggle out of her jeans, and though he tried to look away, his eyes disobeyed. Her panties were black and scanty. *Oh, great!* She cast him an accusing look and he waggled his brows wickedly. Yes, he was definitely a pig. Or a man. Whichever.

"Do you *mind?*"

He shrugged and faced the door, tugging his turtleneck over his head. He heard the bedsprings squeak and knew she'd crawled beneath the covers. "May I turn around?"

"Must you?"

Chuckling, he lay his sweater over the chair back. He kicked one loafer off, then the other, and unzipped his pants. Shucking his slacks, he draped them across the chair seat. "Close your eyes, Miss St. John, I'm turning."

She lay with her back to him, the covers up to her ears, an explicit indication of how accurately he'd read her vibes. "I'm climbing in," he taunted.

"Oh, shut up."

He choked back a laugh and snapped off the light. "Good night, darling."

Her groan held all the overtones of blasphemy. The disgruntled sound affected him with a bothersome combination of amusement and annoyance. Why the hell was he attracted to her, anyway? Why did even their sparring turn him on? Maybe he needed to have his hormone level checked and some of it siphoned off. Clearly there was an imbalance somewhere.

HALLIE WOKE UP to the happy discovery that it had stopped snowing sometime during the night. A fluttery touch on her chin made her glance down. Trisha lay there, cuddled in her arms. A tiny hand explored Hallie's face. "Hi, sweetie," she whispered. "You're being awfully good. Aren't you wet or hungry, or having teething pains?"

Trisha stuck a finger between Hallie's lips and gurgled a smile. Hallie saw a flash of white and put her own finger to the baby's lower lip to get a better look at her gums. "Why, that nasty old tooth broke through! Congratulations on the first of many." Hallie bent to kiss the baby's head. As she did, she noticed something else. A big hand lay across Trisha's pink blanket. A big, *male* hand. That hand was connected to a tanned forearm that stretched all the way across Hallie's body.

Growing more alert, she realized there was much more than a masculine arm encroaching on her personal space. Her whole backside was plastered up against something too solid and hairy to be cast-off pillows.

She jerked her head around to confirm her suspicions and was met by a pair of mischievous blue eyes. "Morning."

She gasped. Her first reaction was to leap from the bed, but she knew she couldn't do that without tossing the baby into the air. As a second choice, she glared her most murderous glare, hissing, "Just what do you think you're doing?"

He came up on one elbow, but didn't remove his arm from her waist. "Not much." He grinned one of those dastardly, breathtaking grins. "Or you wouldn't have to ask."

"This is *reprehensible*. I told you to stay on your side!"

"Of the baby," he reminded her, his expression amused. "I am."

She took a quick survey of the bed and her relative location in it. Good grief! He was right where he should be. She swallowed hard. "Well...but, I mean...how did the baby get over there and how did I get here?"

He lifted the hand that had been across her body and swept a stray lock of hair off his forehead. "I was asleep, sweetheart. This one's on you."

Why, oh, why, did she relish his solid, masculine texture fitted up against her? Why, oh, why, did she want to lay back, snuggle in, bump and grind against him until— Until...

With an irrational combination of belligerence and regret, she struggled to sit, making herself put distance between them. This foolish female fluttering had to stop! This man was her worst nightmare! "However it happened, it was an accident," she insisted breathlessly. "Turn around."

He eyed her narrowly for a moment before he did as she demanded. Careful not to disturb Trisha, she clambered out of the bed and yanked on her jeans. "The highway had better be cleared," she muttered, stomping into her shoes.

"Or what? You'll use force?"

She spun on him. He was sitting up, lounging against the headboard. His chest was broad, the muscles well-defined, with just enough hair to make the view especially...troubling. His expression held a challenge. "You know, Hallie, you can't have everything your way, all the time."

She saw great irony in that statement. "Ha! You should talk! I haven't had anything my way since I found your baby under my Christmas tree!"

"You've had every damn thing your way!" His eyes flashed with sudden anger. "You're here, sweetheart. If you'll recall, nobody asked you to come."

She felt the sting of his accusation. "Well, you're entirely welcome!" she blurted, deeply hurt. "If you think I wanted to come, you're crazy! I was only trying to help. If you can't see that, then—then..." Her voice broke and she had to swallow several times to get control. "Oh, what's the use?" She grabbed the tote bag. "I'm going to change Trisha, then I'd like to get out of here." She pulled out a diaper, then stopped, glaring at him. "No, I won't *interfere*." She tossed the diaper at him and he had to snag it in midair to keep from being smacked in the face.

Hallie tromped around the bed to the door. "Change her yourself. I'll be in the café, having breakfast."

"You could order me something. I'd like pan—"

She slammed out of the room.

6

NATE DIDN'T KNOW how Hallie did it to him, but with everything else he had to worry about today, he kept seeing her wounded expression. All the way home in the silent car, she'd stared straight ahead, eyeing the road with one-hundred-percent concentration.

He couldn't believe that he'd snapped at her like that. Sure, she'd insisted on driving him to Grand Lake—but it had been to avoid the very real possibility of him falling asleep at the wheel and careening off into a ravine. Whatever her plans had been for the past few days, she hadn't been able to accomplish any of them. She'd spent all her time helping him.

He stood in front of her apartment door and frowned. Apologizing wasn't one of his strongest skills. Especially when it meant having to admit he was a jerk. Inhaling with determination, he knocked.

He heard her come to the door, and sensed her peering at him through the peephole. Shoving his hands into his pockets, he stood there feeling like a fly about to be swatted. When the door didn't open, he coaxed, "Hallie? I'd like to talk to you for a minute."

Nothing.

"I don't want you to baby-sit. Honest."

More nothing.

He exhaled, realizing he was going to have to do

a hell of a lot better than he was doing. "I want to apologize. I appreciate everything you've done for me, and I owe you. So, I want you to come to a party I'm giving tonight. There'll be food, and I promise to be on my best behavior." He paused, listening. An excruciating amount of nothing came from her side of the door. "Okay," he muttered. "I'm a pig. Make that a belly-crawling, inconsiderate, putrefying sack of dirt who doesn't deserve to live." He paused, eyeing the peephole with a wry grin. "Am I close?"

After another long pause, a rattling sound drew his glance to the doorknob. It was turning.

Hallie leaned against her doorjamb, her arms crossed in front of her. She'd changed into a white knit shirt and clean jeans. Her hair was damp from a shower. She stared at him with animosity. "Pig works for me," she said.

He cleared his throat, trying to hold his temper. He wasn't used to being called a pig, even if he deserved the title. "Look," he began, "the party is for my employees and a few friends. I'd like you to come. It's the least I can do, considering what you've done for Trisha."

The wrinkle in her brow eased slightly. She opened her mouth to speak, then closed it again. It was clear that his invitation—or at least the sincerity of it—had caught her off guard. He had a feeling she was trying to come up with an excuse.

"I've been thinking about changing bookkeepers," he mentioned casually. Maybe the dangled carrot of a potential client might turn her around. "If you want a shot at the job, it would be good P.R. to come and schmooze with the boss."

Her eyes weren't the angry slits they had been a

minute ago, but they still held quite a bit of reservation. ''Are you really looking for a new book-keeper?''

''Yep.'' He half smiled. Just as he'd expected, she was ambitious and hungry. Appealing to her on a professional level would get him further than appealing to her as a man to a woman.

He watched as Hallie lowered her arms to her sides, looking less belligerent. ''What about Trisha?''

''Goldie Feldick upstairs got back from Oklahoma City yesterday. She insisted on taking Trisha for the rest of the afternoon and during the party.''

Hallie looked pensive.

''She has grandchildren,'' he added, hating the defensive edge to his voice. ''They've stayed with her while her daughter and son-in-law went on vacation.''

''I know.'' Hallie looked at him, her features now almost devoid of animosity. ''I wasn't going to argue. I think Goldie's basically stable. She just has that one, weird hobby.''

''I like Goldie, too.'' It was true, though, that the fifty-something widow *did* have a peculiar interest—conjuring up perfumes from herbs and spices. Today, she'd smelled suspiciously of sausage with a touch of lilac. He checked his watch. ''Look, I have some errands to run. What do you say? Eight o'clock?''

She bit her lower lip, casting her glance away. He gritted his teeth. What else did she want from him? An ear?

After a few ticks of the clock she met his gaze. ''Can I bring anything?''

It surprised him that she accepted. He'd had a gut feeling she would not only refuse but kick him in the shin. He shook his head. ''My secretary's sister is a caterer. I'm getting her Feed The Free World Sampler—if what it's costing me is any indication.''

"You make it sound irresistible."

"You're backing out."

She shook her head. "No. See you at eight." She slipped inside the apartment, and once again he was staring at her door. He felt a strange, benumbed sense of satisfaction—the way he always felt after a dental appointment. Anticipating dental work was much more painful than the reality. This apology had turned out pretty well. He and Hallie were in a good place. They were no longer a battling man and woman; now they were potentially employer and employee.

And *he* would be the boss.

Pleased with himself, Nate headed down the steps, whistling off-key.

HALLIE DIDN'T MEAN to be fashionably late, but for some demented reason, she couldn't decide what to wear. It wasn't as though Nate's party required anything fancy. She probably could have worn jeans. Still, she'd wriggled in and out of so many different outfits, she'd started to feel like one of those runway models. But without the salary or the cheekbones.

Finally she decided to wear what she'd had on at eight-fifteen. The persimmon wool vest was relatively formfitting and hit her a few inches above the knee. The side slits allowed her to walk like a normal person, not somebody in prison-issue ankle chains. Under that she wore a black turtleneck, leggings and ankle boots. "I look like one of Santa's elves," she muttered, pinning a chunky Christmas tree brooch to her lapel—a gift from "her girls."

What difference did it make what she wore? She

wasn't trying to impress the guy, just cover her body to a degree that wouldn't provoke a call to the cops. As for the bookkeeper job he'd tempted her with…well, if leggings put her out of the running— She didn't have much of a shot at it, anyway. Why would he hire her, for Pete's sake? She might as well not get her hopes up about him becoming a client. Besides, would she want Nate Hawksmoor as her boss?

Nate answered her knock as though he'd been standing beside the door. When he saw her, his grin changed somehow, from party-host polite to intent. His gaze roamed over her. "Well, well…" He startled her by taking her hand and pulling her over the threshold. "I thought you'd changed your mind."

She smiled, unable to stop herself. Nate had a way about him, a prodigal charm that refused to be denied. And to make matters worse, he looked wonderful in tailored gray slacks and a blue polo shirt that brought out the color of his eyes. "I didn't change my mind," she said. "I was just working on my appetite. I'm starving."

"Good girl. There's food everywhere. I'm starting to wonder what Europe is doing for eats tonight." He didn't let go of her hand as he led her around, introducing her to his office staff and their spouses. Of course, she'd already met Buffy, who was spilling out of a silky, low-cut, red dress. As Hallie watched, Buffy fed Nate a chip and some dip, then, quite unnecessarily, wiped the corners of his mouth with her napkin. Hallie stifled an urge to roll her eyes.

"And this is my older brother, Henry," Nate was saying. Hallie noticed a family resemblance in Henry's striking eyes. He was an inch or two shorter than Nate, his hair curlier. And he was thinner. He looked somehow depleted, used up, though he couldn't be more than forty. She shook Henry's hand as Nate went on. "And his wife, Nell. Henry, Nell, this is the lady who helped me with Trisha. My neighbor, Hallie St. John."

Nell brushed Henry's hand away from Hallie's and inserted her own. "How do you do, Hallie?" she said. The woman was tall, dark and pretty, but her face had an unattractive hardness to it, especially around the mouth. "I never liked that Viv, not one bit. I told Nate a thousand times to get rid of the little snip, but you know men! Their brains are all in their—" She broke off, eyeing her husband sharply. "Henry, didn't I tell you not to eat any more of that liver pâté. You know you're allergic. I won't have you keeping me awake snoring when your nasal passages swell up."

She pulled her manicured fingers from Hallie's hand, grabbed the cracker spread with the offending pâté and popped it into her own mouth. "You eat the celery," she said between chews. "You need the roughage." Turning back to Hallie, Nell made a disgusted face. "If I don't keep my eye on him every minute, he…" She sighed theatrically and fussed with her husband's shirt collar. "He's such a *child,* but then, aren't all men?"

Hallie was a touch shell-shocked by the woman's harangue. With a confused nod, she responded, "Well, I, uh…"

"Excuse us. Hallie hasn't met everyone," Nate said, his voice tight. As he steered her away, Hallie caught another fleeting glimpse of Henry, his eyes downcast. That poor man—brow-beaten and belittled by his wife. She glanced at Nate and discovered he was watching her. He raised an eyebrow. "Like her?"

Hallie shrugged, not wanting to disparage a relative, though she had a feeling Nate would agree with the worst possible description she might put to his sister-in-law.

"Henry married a woman just like the woman who married dear old dad," he said wryly.

She eyed Nate, light dawning. "I'm beginning to see why you choose the women you do."

With his hand at her elbow, he halted her. "Can you blame me?"

She smiled wanly. "No, but—" She stopped herself. What was she going to say? That leaping to the opposite extreme wasn't the answer, either? Didn't she feel the same way about men as he did about women? Didn't she choose the "I'll do anything you say Snookims" kind of guy? Who was she to tell him how to live his life?

"But what?" he asked, pulling her back.

She blinked, refreshed her smile. "Nothing." She had a sudden sense that she needed some distance. He was too stimulating, this guy who wanted only fawning bimbettes in his life. She didn't want to be so aware of him—of his scent, his touch. Indicating the dining room table, nearly buckling under the weight of delectable eatables, she asked, "Mind if I graze?"

When he released her arm, she experienced both relief and regret, but worked to maintain a nonchalant facade.

"Go for it." His grin turned teasing. "Make yourself sick."

"Charmingly put," she flung back, wishing she

didn't enjoy sparring with him so much. "For you, I'll try."

He laughed, the sound sending an unruly thrill through her. She turned away, which was a chore. Those dratted eyes had a way of capturing her and holding her against her will.

A hot blush warmed her cheeks as she rushed to the table and scooped up a crackerful of something blue. She took a bite. It was good, for blue food. She chewed, forcing her mind to other things. Concentrating hard, she scanned Nate's guests as they milled around, chatted, or laughed in little human pods in front of the blazing hearth. She calculated there were around two dozen people here, all young, all attractive, all intelligent-looking.

Her gaze fell on Nate's brother, and her heart constricted. His wife was spitting on a napkin and rubbing at a spot on his gray pullover. Poor, poor man. How humiliating to be treated like a two-year-old in front of everybody. But if Nate's remark was accurate, the two brothers had grown up watching their father being treated the same way. Interestingly, Henry had accepted it as the way of the world, no matter how miserable it made him.

On the other hand, Nate had witnessed the same mistreatment of his father and decided not to let himself get caught up in the same hopeless trap. That was why he chose women he could control. And why *she* picked men she could handle.

Scooping out another bite of the blue dip, she chanced a peek at Nate. He was dancing with Buffy, her *Cosmo*-mussed-to-perfection head resting against his chest. A few other couples were slow-dancing. Luckily, he didn't have a great deal of furniture in his living room. She shifted her gaze. Watching Buffy nuzzle Nate irritated her.

Turning her back, Hallie focused her attention on the boiled shrimp. Delicious. Next she ate a tangy cocktail wiener, then sampled a bite of the nutty cheese ball. She certainly had no complaints about the food. If she put her mind to it, she really could make herself sick, by taking even just one bite of everything.

"Oh, well…" she sighed, dipping up another chipful of the yummy blue goop. "I'm here to eat Nate's food, not to make value judgments."

"Excuse me?"

She jumped at the sound of Nate's voice.

"What?" she squeaked, inhaling a bit of blue stuff and choking.

"I thought you spoke to me," he said over her coughing.

She coughed and gasped for air, shaking her head.

"I'd pat your back, but I read someplace that can make it worse."

She held up a halting hand, straining to breathe. She didn't want him to pat her back. She didn't even want him to watch! Why, oh, why, couldn't he still be on the other side of the room doing the bump-and-rub with Buffy?

"If you want me to start the Heimlich, let me know."

Her eyes watered and she gasped, sucking in, longing for a breath of air.

"Just nod." He looked worried.

She sucked in again; this time air made it all the way to her lungs. With a huge inhale, she closed her eyes. "It—it's okay…" she gasped at last.

"That's good news," he said. "I like my guests to live through the whole party."

She opened her eyes to discover he was holding a red napkin toward her. She snatched it, wiping at the tears. "Thanks," she whispered through a painful wheeze.

"It's the least I can do." He smiled warmly. She hated it when he did that. It made her knees weak, and she was already wobbly from lack of oxygen.

Clearing her throat, she wadded the napkin in her fist. "I think I'll live, now. You can go back to...to whatever you were doing."

His smile didn't dim. "Okay." He held out his hand.

She looked at him, puzzled.

"I was about to ask you to dance."

She swallowed. *"Me?"*

His grin broadened, making her heart flip-flop stupidly. *Rotten, rotten, cruel bum!* "I claim the host's right to dance with each of my female guests." He inclined his head as though in question. "Didn't you read that in the small print of your invitation?"

Something prickled along her spine. She was afraid it was anticipation of being held in his arms. How did she plan to get out of this? "Uh, we, uh-mmm..." *Brilliant, Hallie! Real pithy!*

"I'll take that as a yes." He pulled her into his arms. "Try not to hold me too close," he teased. "Buffy's watching."

She eyed him dubiously as he led her into a slow dance. "I'm sure if you call for help, someone will rescue you."

He laughed, pulling her a fraction closer. They

were almost touching, but not quite. "I feel safer already."

Experiencing a prickle of petulance, she asked, "If you're so worried, why did you ask me to dance?"

"I like living on the edge."

"Your idea of living on the edge is dancing with me?"

"You're scary."

She frowned. "What you mean is, I intimidate you because I have a mind of my own."

"Like I said." He winked, the act sexy and disconcerting. "You're scary."

His hand at her back felt warm, gentle; his scent was hypnotic. She was enjoying his nearness more than she ought to, considering the confrontational tone of their conversation. With effort, she edged away slightly, deciding to be all business—lay his job offer out in the open for a solid yes or no. "So, Mr. Hawksmoor, do you hire scary women as bookkeepers?"

"Absolutely. I just don't sleep with them." His grin growing lopsided, he bent closer. "Except during blizzards."

His lips brushed her ear and her body reacted strongly, tingling and growing hot. She swallowed, unable to find a meaty retort. If the truth were told, she could hardly breathe.

"Give me the names of a few of your clients for references," he said softly. "My offer was sincere."

When she lifted her gaze to his, he smiled.

"Okay," she whispered.

He held her gaze as they swayed to the music. Her breathing grew rapid under the intensity of his stare. Somewhere deep inside, Hallie knew he'd pulled her close. Or had she been the one to move? Her hand on his shoulder had somehow crept almost to his nape. As they danced, she felt muscle flex under her hand. He was warm, strong, male. She grew dizzy, almost giddy.

He grinned at her and she grinned back. Her physical awareness of him was painfully acute. She knew that was a bad thing, yet for some reason, she continued to gaze into his twinkling eyes. She even found herself lifting her chin, tilting her head just so.

His face seemed nearer, his lips hovering.

Hovering.

She knew she should do something—bob and weave, or better yet, break and run—but her body disobeyed. He was so warm, so invitingly solid. They danced very close, his mouth poised just above hers.

He was going to kiss her! And she was going to kiss him back!

No! No! Her good sense cried, all too quickly drowned out by her weak, stupid female side, cajoling, *Yes! Oh—yes!*

"Nate, honey," came Buffy's shrill voice. "Do you know what's in the crab dip? It's scrump-dilly-icious."

The strange spell was broken by Buffy's inane question. Hallie peeked at Nate as he faced Buffy.

"Crab," Nate said. "Cream cheese or sour—"

"Crab!" Buffy said, and spun away. "You were right, Marvin," she called across the room. "It *is* crab."

Hallie bit her lip to keep from giggling, but a titter escaped.

"Don't be so quick to laugh," Nate muttered in an aside, drawing her gaze. "If Ol' Buddy Sugar Burger is any example, you've done a little boy toy shopping at Airheads-R-Us, too.''

She swallowed the remnants of her giggle and put on a straight face. So Nate thought Sugar was her lover. She supposed that was for the best. After what almost happened when they danced, she needed to put as many stumbling blocks between them as possible. A big teddy bear of a lover was a pretty good deterrent to most guys. She faced him straight-on. ''Sugar is a dear, sweet man.''

Nate pulled her into his arms again, apparently deciding to resume their dance. ''I'm sure he is.''

She allowed him to lead her to the soft, slow strains of the music, wishing she'd taken the opportunity to put distance between them when she'd had the chance. Surely there was a knot of people somewhere in the room in which she could hide. She didn't even care if Buffy was in the knot and the topic of discussion was, ''How much does it cost to send off for free catalogs?''

''You're frowning,'' Nate murmured, breaking into her reverie. ''Did I step on your toe?''

She blinked. ''I was thinking it's some other female guest's turn to dance with you.''

His lips twitched. ''Miss St. John, if you don't want to dance with me, just say so.''

Irritated with herself for feeling at home in his arms, she retorted, ''I don't want to dance with you, Mr. Hawksmoor.''

He stopped moving, but didn't release her. One brow rose and his teeth flashed in a grin. ''Was that so hard?'' He let her go and stepped away.

She stared after him, watching as he placed an arm

around another of his female guests and pulled her into a dance.

So much for breaking his spirit!

She whirled away and nearly crashed into a young man who had come up behind her. He asked her to dance and she accepted. After all, it was a party. Nate Hawksmoor wasn't the only man here.

7

IT SEEMED AS THOUGH every time Hallie saw Nate he was dancing with Buffy. Apparently he'd made the rounds of female guests and returned to his doormat of choice.

Finally, after eating all she could hold, she determined she'd had enough of the spectacle of Buffy dangling from Nate's neck like an overgrown Barbie doll. It was nearly midnight, anyway. Other guests were leaving, so her departure wouldn't seem unduly rushed. When the current belly-rubbing song ended, she took the opportunity to approach Nate and offer a polite goodbye. She plastered on a smile. "It was a lovely party," she said. "Thanks for the invitation. I tried to eat my share." Taking a step backward, she prepared for her escape.

Buffy gave Hallie a narrow–eyed once-over without releasing Nate's arm.

He appeared surprised. What had he expected— that she would offer to stay and wash dishes? "Look…" He lightly took hold of her arm to halt her retreat. "I know this is an imposition, but would you mind getting Trisha for me? I promised Goldie I'd fetch her by midnight, but people are leaving and I need to play host."

He wasn't smiling, his expression was dashingly urgent. Compassion stirred inside her along with a rush of excitement about seeing little Trisha. Plainly, the baby had wangled her way into Hallie's heart, the diabolical darling. For that very reason, she shouldn't go, mustn't allow herself to be swept further into the infant's insidious web of affection.

She gave Buffy a pointed look, as if to say, "Why not let your love slave do it?" Her glance returned to Nate's face. He, too, flicked a look at Buffy. Seemingly oblivious, she smoothed her dress so that it draped just so over her hips. "Unfortunately, Buffy has to be at work early in the morning. She was just telling me she has to leave."

Buffy glanced at Nate and smiled, brushing an imaginary crumb off his shirt. She faced Hallie and her smile hardened. "Yes, Nate is such a sweetie to give his employees the whole week off. It sucks bigtime that winter is such a busy season at Okla-Tan-A-Rama. We're booked solid, starting at seven sharp." She yawned, covering her mouth with her hand. Hallie noticed her fingernails were black, or maybe some funky hue of purple. The polish was probably called something like Smashed In A Car Door.

Hallie eyed the woman with distaste. *You little weasel*, she snapped via ESP. *You can't be holding out hope that Nate will give his daughter away as if she were the last of a litter of puppies!* Rather than voice her theory, she smiled with effort. "Those important winter tans must be attended to." Glancing at Nate, she shrugged, her jaws clamped together. "I'll get Trisha." Darn! She hated herself for weakening. That child was *not* her business. Why didn't Nate send somebody else? As soon as the thought materialized, she knew it was silly. Goldie wouldn't hand over the baby to a stranger.

Nate smiled, obviously grateful for her offer, however reluctantly given. "Thanks." He winked. "I'll send some shrimp home with you. I noticed you liked it."

She flushed. So what if she'd downed a good half pound all by herself? She smirked. "Throw in some of that blue stuff and it's a deal."

He laughed, a deep rich sound that did things to her. Melty things. "You drive a hard bargain, Miss St. John."

Buffy lifted her arms to take his face between her hands. As she pulled his mouth toward hers for a suck-face good-night kiss, Hallie whirled away. She didn't care to ogle. Another thing she didn't care about was the shrimp and the blue food. Darn her hide, she'd longed for an excuse to see Trisha again. Sweetening the deal by demanding the blue dip made it sound like a chore, but she wasn't kidding herself. She was getting sappy over that baby. She didn't care to face that fact, so she rationalized—with Buffy's early morning tanning salon crisis, there was little choice but to help.

She would do this—*one last time.*

She wondered if that's what chain-smokers muttered as they tore into a pack of cigarettes after vowing to quit for the one hundredth time. Scurrying out Nate's door, she tried to squelch another unpalatable notion. Yet even her best efforts couldn't keep the unwelcome conviction from invading her brain. She just might be falling for Trisha's daddy.

In the hallway, she slumped against the wall. Breathing deeply, she mumbled, "That is such a deranged mental malfunction, Hallie St. John, I refuse to dwell on it, not even for an instant. I am not falling for that macho control freak!''

Thirty minutes later Hallie tapped on Nate's door, a precious baby sleeping in her arms. She hadn't meant to linger so long upstairs, but Goldie was quite a talker. Hallie dreaded facing Nate again tonight. Still, she'd made him a promise. Anxious to get this last chore over, she raised a hand to knock again just as the door swung wide.

''Hi.'' Nate stepped out of her way. ''I thought you'd decided to keep Trisha.''

Unhappily, the idea wasn't totally foreign to her. ''Goldie had to tell me all about Christmas with her flawless son, Ferdie Feldick, his good-for-nothing wife, and all the perfect little Feldicks—Frankie, Felicia, Fern, and the twins. I forget their names.''

''Don't tell me,'' he said, through a rumble of amusement. ''But I bet they start with an *F*.''

''How do you do it?'' She smiled in spite of her determination to keep her mind on the job at hand, then get quickly away from the troubling Hawksmoor clan.

''It was a hard choice, deciding between becoming an architect or a psychic,'' he replied.

''Really? Which did you choose?''

''Very funny.''

She looked around. The place was quiet, not a soul in sight. It surprised her to realize Nate was alone. Even the caterers had vanished, along with all evidence of their existence. ''My goodness,'' she said in a hushed voice. ''When your party's over, it's over.''

''Just as well. I didn't sleep much last night.''

She flinched at the reminder and her cheeks burned.

Neither had *she*—except for that unfortunate period when she'd fallen into that bizarre comatose state and crawled into Nate's arms!

She whisked Trisha to her brand-new crib, which resided in a baby-proof corner of the bedroom Nate used as his home office. She had a feeling he would have to look for an apartment with three bedrooms fairly soon. Which meant he wouldn't be in this building much longer. *Which was a good thing,* she assured herself vehemently.

Hallie tucked Trisha under the covers, then remained bent over the crib for another minute, gazing at her. Light from a streetlamp outside the window made Trisha look like the angel she was. Her little thumb was stuck between cherubic lips. Gently, Hallie slipped the tiny appendage from Trisha's mouth, covering the chubby hand with the baby blanket.

An unruly urge overcame her and she kissed her own fingertips and placed them on the baby's cheek. "'Night, little one," she whispered around a lump in her throat. Hurriedly she turned away. Walking out of the room, she promised herself that she would now move on with her life. In the future, she would leave Nathan Hawksmoor and his daughter to their own devices. She was well out of it.

She leaned against the wall outside the bedroom and eyed the ceiling. With a long exhale, she repeated her promise. "You're going to walk out that door and bid father and daughter a brisk goodbye!"

"Coffee?"

Her gaze flew toward the living room. Nate stood behind the couch that faced the fireplace. He held two steaming mugs. Lifting them, as if for emphasis, he added, "Don't worry. It's decaf."

No. Not on your life, buddy boy! I'm leaving this instant. She pushed away from the wall and entered the living room. *You're not fast-talking me or charming me into anything—not even a cup of decaf coffee! I'm outta here!*

It shocked her to find herself seated beside him on the sofa, accepting a mug from his hands. "Thanks," she said, her voice oddly husky.

He took a sip. "Did Goldie have any problems with Trisha?"

Hallie shook her head. "No, but when I picked her up, she smelled like...well, I can only describe it as raspberry ragout. I presume it's one of Goldie's latest perfumes."

His grin flashed, heart-stopping in the firelight. "Probably. Her aftershaves have more oregano."

In the quiet room their laughter mingled with the crackling of the fire—a pleasant moment. He sat his mug on the table and relaxed. There was something lazily seductive about his movements, and Hallie suddenly found it hard to breathe. Sipping her coffee, she strove to feel total indifference toward the man.

"Did you have a good time tonight?" he asked, his gaze radiant with firelight.

She nodded, reluctantly feasting on his muscular physique as he lounged there. His posture was utterly nonthreatening, yet there was something alarming, even dangerous, about him.

"Good." He draped an arm across the back of the couch, his thumb brushing her shoulder. "I've felt bad all day about being sharp with you this morning. You've been a great help to me when I needed it. I don't know what I would have done without you."

She took another sip of her coffee while her brain

scolded, *Say goodbye! Get up and leave! Tell him to quit that sneaky smiling and underhanded smelling good!* She placed her cup beside his on the coffee table and sat back to stare into the fire.

She felt his forearm, warm against her back. *Run, stupid woman! Run!*

"Hallie?"

She blinked, startled to discover she'd been sitting motionless and mute for heaven only knew how long. When she turned to face him, her heart did a wild flip-flop. He'd leaned toward her, evidently concerned by her overlong silence. They were awfully close, almost lip to lip. She opened her mouth to speak, but no words came.

To her complete shock and dismay, she found herself shifting forward and kissing him.

Kissing *him!*

Without thinking, with the casualness of blowing out a match, she simply kissed the man. But in this case, the slight pucker of her lips didn't blow out a flame. It ignited one.

She sensed Nate's initial surprise. But before her horror and embarrassment could turn to humiliation, he was kissing her back. His arm, which had been resting on the sofa back, came around her. His other hand slipped to the small of her back, fingers spread, pulling her close.

The strong hardness of his mouth sent the pit of her stomach into a frenzied spin. She grew weak. Moaning against his lips, she encircled him with her arms, hugging with all her might.

He moved his mouth across hers, devouring, stoking a fire in her that had been simmering, uninvited for days. The touch of his lips sang through her veins.

His kiss grew more persuasive, hungrier, coaxing her lips to part so he could explore more fully, incite more passionately.

The intimacy of the deepened kiss sent shivers of yearning dashing through her. She met him thrust for thrust, their tongues dancing, teasing, seeking and finding. His hands moved gently, tantalizing with feather-light touches, and a sizzling craving, an aching need, built within her.

Without warning, she found herself beneath him, relishing the powerful, solid length of him stretched over her. She hugged his hips with her legs, held him in intimate captivity.

His low groan made her giddy with power and she smiled against his mouth. Feeling reckless, she could think about nothing else, care about nothing else, but bringing this man to his knees. Nate was a commanding male, master of his destiny, lord of his castle. But she would make him whimper at her feet. Lifting her lips away, she nipped at his mouth, then trailed kisses along his jaw to his ear. She flicked her tongue strategically and was rewarded with another guttural moan.

Mad with power, Hallie tugged on his shirt, pulling it out of his waistband, up and over his head. His marvelous torso was hers to fondle, lick, suckle. She had spent a lot of energy fighting wild fantasies about Nate's chest, ever since last night at Erma's Place when he'd rid himself of his shirt in front of her. She'd itched to feel the rough chest hair against her breasts. "Undress me, Nate," she coaxed, flicking her tongue into his ear to taunt him. "Unless you're afraid to find out just how scary I can be."

He lifted his head, his eyes hot with passion. "Is

that a dare, Miss St. John?'' he asked, his voice pleasingly rough.

She wasn't sure what it was, but there was no help for that now. Her body thrummed with need for the virile male animal in her arms. Burying her face against his throat, she kissed, nipped, licked, ran her nails up and down his bare back to tantalize, excite. ''Are you man enough?'' she taunted, ''to take on a real woman?''

He growled, shifting to sit up. Her legs were still wrapped around his waist, so she ended up squarely in his lap. She giggled at the dizzying flight. Even before she recovered, he unbuttoned her vest and slipped it off her arms. ''I'll show you who's man enough, sweetcakes,'' he whispered, tugging her turtleneck over her head. ''You'll be purring like a kitten in a few minutes.''

''Not too few, I hope,'' she murmured with a come-on smile, watching his gaze linger on the black lace of her bra. The hook lay between her breasts. His hands came up, and she expected him to unfasten the bra, cast it aside. Instead, warm hands cupped her. Lowering his face, he kissed the exposed skin, making her gasp. She closed her eyes with the sensations of pleasure his mouth elicited.

He slid his tongue beneath the edging of her bra and she sighed, long and languidly. If his strong arms hadn't encircled her, she might have fallen backward. ''You're already purring, sweetheart,'' he said against her flesh. A victorious chuckle rode his tone.

Her eyes snapped wide and she sat bolt upright, pressing him away. ''I'll show you who'll be purring.'' Her grin wily, she proceeded to unfasten his belt buckle.

Hours later, Hallie and Nate lay entwined in front of the embers of a dying fire. Somehow, during the tumultuous lovemaking, a comforter had been introduced into the mix, so instead of the Oriental rug, they lay tangled in each other's arms on down-filled cotton.

Though the room was dark, Hallie's eyes had adjusted to the dimness. Nate slept with one arm across her waist, his hand cupping her bottom. Except for size and texture, their legs were so intertwined an observer would be hard-pressed to tell whose legs belonged to whom.

Hallie's cheeks burned at the thought of an observer. She and Nate had done things to each other and for each other...things that weren't meant for an audience. Unable to help herself, she traced a hand along his upper arm, the contour of muscle so tempting, so stimulating.

She felt herself becoming aroused again and tried to quash the feeling. She was no nymphomaniac. She'd never made a sexual glutton of herself before, but Nate certainly knew how to make a woman glad she was a woman. She'd never known such a complete sense of gratification in her life. Making love with Nate was beautiful and natural, as it was doubtless meant to be. And from the groaning and moaning he'd done, she sensed he wasn't exactly unsatisfied, either.

He stirred, and she realized she'd been running her hand along his chest, luxuriating in the tactile sensations of crisp hair and solid muscle beneath her fingertips. Her gaze shot to his face. He was smiling at her. "Was I snoring?"

"No." She smiled, experiencing a swell of completeness, of a contentment she didn't deserve and shouldn't be feeling!

He lifted a brow. "Is there something you want?"

She snuggled closer, slipping her hand along his waist to his back. "Mmm-hmm."

"What?" he whispered. "A glass of water?"

"No."

With a husky laugh, he squeezed her hip affectionately. "Let me think."

"You do that." She kissed his collarbone, mindful of how her soft curves molded perfectly to the hard contours of his body—like two puzzle pieces coming together to complete a long-sought image.

He pressed her hips into his groin. She was treated with a delightful indication that he not only knew what she wanted, but was well equipped to oblige. "I'm afraid I can't even guess what you want."

Suddenly so hot for him that she was beyond playing games, Hallie let out a growl and pressed him to his back.

NATE WOKE UP with an overpowering sense of remorse. What the hell had he done? He looked at the woman cuddled within his embrace, her nakedness a guilty reminder of his lapse last night. Hallie wasn't the kind of woman he was looking for; Buffy was his type.

He knew if he'd given his girlfriend an ultimatum either to stay with him last night or get out of his life, she would have stayed and he would have been in control.

So how had everything gone wrong? Why the hell hadn't he insisted that Buffy stay? The tanning salon was only ten minutes away. He could have gotten her there this morning. Why in blazes had he asked Hallie to get Trisha? Why had he offered her coffee? And most curious of all, why had he been happier to have the pushy woman, with a mind of her own, alone with him after the party?

He hadn't planned a seduction. He hadn't planned anything, really. Which was unlike him. Usually he had his life planned down to the smallest detail. He only knew Hallie irritated him and delighted him and exasperated him and excited him. When she'd surprised him with that kiss, his common sense had exploded into useless bits.

Thinking about that kiss wasn't productive. It only made him want her again. Instinctively, he kissed the top of her head, regretting it as soon as it was done. What was his problem? He'd made a bad mistake last night—several times.

Just because it suited Hallie to fetch Trisha last night and just because it suited her to have sex with him, momentarily forgetting Sugar, only proved her independent nature would never work for him.

She sighed in her sleep and snuggled deeper into the curve of his body. He winced, squeezing his eyes shut as he struggled to hold himself in check. *Damn it.* The woman didn't know what she was doing to him.

He'd never had better sex in his life. That was one thing he could say for an assertive woman. She didn't hesitate to do what she felt. She showed him some things about being scary, all right. She was beautifully scary sexually. He would be perfectly happy to never leave this spot—to just make love to her over and over until they both died happily from exhaustion.

Sadly, life didn't work that way. He couldn't dwell

on what they'd shared during the night. His mistake had to be rectified. He had to nip this impossible situation in the bud. His first impulse was to shake her awake, then quickly move out of touching distance. But he didn't shake her awake, and he didn't move away. He lingered, inhaling, taking in her fragrance. Clean. Light. Like distant roses and freshly cut grass.

The scent made him feel strangely happy, as though it conjured up a good childhood memory. He breathed deeply, wondering what the memory was, trying to bring it to the surface. Roses and freshly cut grass. Ah, yes. The Richmonds. He remembered now. They had been a middle-aged couple who'd lived down the block from his home. To avoid his mother's constant haranguing, he'd often escaped on his skateboard. Many a Saturday he'd found himself in the Richmonds' front yard, chatting with the couple while Mrs. Richmond tended her roses and Mr. Richmond cut the grass.

At the time he'd thought them odd but special people. Mrs. Richmond would say to her husband, ''Darling, could you please fetch me a glass of tea?'' and Mr. Richmond would quickly, even eagerly, oblige her. This didn't seem so unusual to Nate. He'd spent his life listening to his mother make demands of his father and watching the man do her bidding. But the stunning thing to Nate had been when Mr. Richmond said to his wife, ''Love, would you mind getting me my straw hat?'' And she would rise from the garden and do as he asked, smiling and humming all the while.

They were so accommodating and good-natured in their attitude toward doing for each other. Nate had been confused, wondering who was in control. Neither seemed to be. He frowned in thought. How did such seemingly even-handed relationships happen? Or did his childish eyes and ears miss some subtle sign of dominance? That must have been it.

Still as he inhaled Hallie's essence, his heart was lighter than it should have been, considering the circumstances.

Enough! He was stalling, pure and simple. He had to act. Put her out of his thoughts, his apartment and his life. With renewed firmness, he propped himself up on one elbow and grasped her shoulder. "Hallie," he said. "Wake up."

She stirred and made a mewling sound that made it plain she didn't relish being awakened at five-thirty in the morning. But Trisha would be yelling with hunger by six. Nate had to get this over and done. "Hallie, sweetcakes..." He gritted his teeth at his offhand tone, but it was necessary to sound casual. "Daylight's burning."

She opened her eyes and shifted onto her back. She smiled, lifting her arms to encircle his neck. "Hi." Her voice was dreamy, her eyelids making a charming effort to stay open. "Kiss me?"

He stifled a shiver of desire. Kissing her, making wild love to her, was the *only* thing he wanted to do. Gazing at her there, sleepy, vulnerable, and sexy, was a risky undertaking, eroding his resolve.

Clearing his throat, he made himself remove her arms from his neck and he sat up. "I feel like pancakes for breakfast," he informed her with believable indifference. Standing, he extracted his gaze from her naked beauty. "I like my coffee strong, sweetcakes." Turning his back, he strode away, delivering his coup de grâce. "I'll take a shower while you fix it."

He knew as well as he knew his own name that by the time he came out of the bathroom, Hallie would be gone. That was good. She wouldn't like him much, but it was the only way to handle the situation. What a shame he'd made the stupid mistake of getting to know her sexually. That knowledge would work against him if he tried to stay on friendly terms with her. He couldn't leave it at this one-night stand. He'd have to have her in his life.

Sex, however, wasn't all there was to a relationship. Sooner or later one of them would have to have the upper hand and they'd split. Their basic needs in a relationship were simply too contrary for anything long-term.

He soaped himself, then pressed his palms against the cool tile wall. Soaking beneath the warm water, washing away Hallie's scent, Nate wished it were as easy to wash away the erotic memories she'd engraved on his brain. He noticed with great regret that he was becoming aroused.

With a raw curse he twisted off the hot water tap. A cold shower was what he needed to blast lusty thoughts of—

Bang! The shower stall door crashed open. Before Nate could react he was pelted with globs of a white substance along with a blinding cloud of black specks.

"Here are your pancakes, sweetcheeks," Hallie snapped. "And do let me know if the coffee's strong enough."

The door slammed shut. Half-blinded, Nate stood stock-still, encrusted with what he guessed was an entire box of pancake mix and a pound of ground coffee.

He squinted down at himself, watching the muck slither along his body. He hadn't expected this.

Slumping against the wall, he wiped a chunk of pancake mix out of one eye. A rush of incongruous humor quirked his lips. There was not a submissive bone in that woman's body. He couldn't fault her for what she'd done to him, though. Hadn't he practically begged for it?

His fledgling grin died when he recalled the look of hurt in her eyes as she'd yanked open the shower door. "Congratulations, Nate. Your scheme worked," he mumbled, ducking beneath the frigid spray. "Aren't you the clever bastard."

8

By noon, Hallie was still furious with Nate. An unexpected advantage of her anger was that it helped suppress her pain and sense of loss—at least for now. *How dare he! How dare he!* Slamming out of her apartment, she hurried along the hall to the stairs. Taking them two at a time to the first floor, she marched out the security door to the entry alcove and its six apartment mailboxes.

The cut-glass ovals in the double entry revealed a light fluttering of snow falling across the treed side street. She paused, staring out, though her mind wasn't on the sight in front of her. Miserable, she pressed her forehead against the cold glass and closed her eyes. Lord, Nate had hurt her. She hadn't realized how deeply one offhand comment about breakfast could slash. But she'd bled then and she was bleeding now.

Her nose tingled, and she feared she was going to burst into silly sobs. *No! Don't let go, Hallie! You brought this on yourself.*

Wiping at a tear, she straightened her shoulders and resolved to get on with her life, putting soft memories of Nate's lovemaking out of it. Retrieving her mail, she thumbed through it, forcing herself to pay attention. A bill, junk, a bill, junk, junk…

She headed back through the security door and up

the steps. As she reached her apartment, Nate's door opened. Reflexively she looked his way, then wished she'd had the presence of mind to ignore him. He stopped dead, obviously as uncomfortable by the chance meeting as she.

Unable to help herself, she looked him up and down. In pressed jeans and a black cashmere turtleneck, he looked cuddly and sexy, and disgruntled.

He nodded without smiling. "Hi."

She lifted her chin in what she hoped was a disdainful response. She heard a muffled clatter and realized several pieces of her mail had fallen to the floor. *Oh, fine!* Her attempt at superior contempt would be badly diluted by a show of fidgety clumsiness.

She crouched to retrieve the fallen envelopes at the same instant he did. He touched her electric bill, but she swatted his hand away. *"Don't!"*

His glance shot to hers. The expression in his eyes seemed sad for a split second. Or had she imagined it? Now she saw nothing but remoteness. His lips twisted humorlessly. "Whatever the lady wants."

She eyed him angrily, her pain bubbling to the surface. "How did you like your breakfast?"

He grimaced. "It gave me a rash." He stood abruptly.

The wry confession surprised her so completely she felt like laughing. As she rose, she unsuccessfully maintained a straight face. A peek at him told her he hadn't missed her smirk. Good! He deserved to suffer, the overbearing jerk. What monumental conceit, thinking that just because they'd made beautiful love—er, had passable sex—she would instantly become his groveling love slave!

His obvious anxiety bolstered her courage and she eyed him directly. "It's ironic how twenty-four short hours ago, we both agreed you were a pig."

His frown deepened. "Ironic?"

"Ironic," she echoed, working to keep her voice from breaking. "We were *criminally* flattering to you."

His eyes narrowed, and she was surprised he didn't turn and stalk away. "I try to put my best foot forward," he said at last.

His caustic wit made her smile scornfully. She had to give him credit. He had an excellent grasp of sarcasm. "Your best foot, huh? That must have been the kick I felt this morning."

He shoved his hands into his pockets. "You can kick pretty good, yourself, sweetheart." He scratched his chest, making his point.

She gritted her teeth. Evidently he had no intention of apologizing today! So this was how he operated. He acted the gentleman, seduced with soft firelight and decaf coffee, then if the woman didn't immediately fall into step three paces behind him, he booted her out the door without even a "Thanks for the exercise."

"Look," he said, his features solemn. "Let's not let personal feelings get in the way of our working together. If you'll get me those references—"

"Working together!" she cut in, horrified. Glaring daggers, she counted to ten to keep from attacking him bodily and choking him for his insensitivity. "Mr. Hawksmoor, if you were the last man on earth, I wouldn't touch your books!" How cold—how callous—could he be? Did he really expect her to work for him after...after—

With a moan that turned into a growl, she shoved at his chest. Caught off guard, he stumbled a step backward. "I do not get jobs by sleeping with men," she asserted. "Don't throw me crumbs! As far as I'm concerned, last night didn't happen and you don't exist! If you have an ounce of conscience, you'll avoid even making eye contact with me. Is that clear?"

He stared at her for an overlong moment, then lifted his chin in a curt half nod. "Crystal." His jaw bunching, he glanced toward the stairs.

Hallie heard the scrape of footsteps and turned to look in the same direction. As she watched, a tall, black Stetson appeared, sparkling with melting snow. The shaded face of Wayne Sugarbush appeared as he mounted the next step. When he saw Hallie and Nate, his face lit up in a toothy grin.

From his expression, it was apparent Sugar hadn't heard the argument. Hallie breathed a relieved sigh. With a surge of emotion that was no small part the desire for revenge, she rushed into the cowboy's arms. With a whoop, she squealed, "I didn't expect you back this week!" Good old Sugar. He was an easygoing friend. He would make her feel better.

A spiteful imp in her brain whispered, *Even better, Nate will think your lover is back.* If only the notion would grind his insides to dust! Even if it didn't, letting Nate think there were men in the world who sought her out made Hallie feel slightly less broken and discarded.

"Darlin'," Sugar drawled, whirling her around as she dangled from his neck. "You make a guy feel mighty welcome on such a gray winter day."

Sugar caught her up in his arms with the ease of hefting a five-pound bag of potatoes. Striding forward, he gave Nate a nod. Hallie eyed Nate, too, but her smile was a frozen fake. It pricked her when he didn't meet her gaze.

"Hi, there, ol' buddy," Sugar said, still holding Hallie in his arms. "How's tricks?"

Hallie flinched at the unfortunate word choice. She watched Nate for signs of distress, but he merely lifted one eyebrow, a smile easing onto his lips. Experiencing a melancholy flurry of memories of everything those lips could do, she wrenched her gaze from his mouth.

"How's it shakin', Wayne?" Nate asked, sounding at ease.

Sugar's guffaw filled the hallway. "Too cold to shake, ol' buddy." He squeezed Hallie with open affection. "But my best gal here'll take care of that. Right, darlin'?"

She presented Sugar with her most radiant smile. "Don't I always?" she practically cooed.

Nate cleared his throat and bent to retrieve the envelopes Hallie had scattered in her mad dash to her trucker. After gathering her mail, he stood and held it out to her. "Nice to see you, Miss St. John."

She took his offering, her gaze severe, sending a private message about exactly how thrilled she was to see him, too. "Why, thank you, Mr. Hawksmoor," she intoned. "Gentlemanly behavior is so rare these days."

He watched her for several heartbeats, his eyelids at half-mast, his lashes casting shadows on his cheeks. She couldn't read his thoughts, but had a feeling if she was running for office, he'd drop dead before he gave her his vote. Nate's glance moved to Sugar and he indicated the direction of the steps. "I need to get my mail. Excuse me?"

"Sure, sure." Sugar grinned at Hallie. "Got anything in that apartment to warm up a frozen ol' country boy?"

From her elevated position, she reached down to turn the doorknob. "Not just warm, Sugar. It'll make you *hot*." She peeked at Nate's back as he strolled toward the stairs. She wanted badly to see him stumble to his knees with green-eyed jealousy, or at the very least, exhibit a shiver of envy. Nothing. He merely strolled away as though he'd forgotten they both existed.

Sugar, of course, knew Hallie had been talking about her famous five-alarm chili, not hot sex. But if Hallie could help it, Nate would *never* know that! As a matter of fact, she planned to make sure Nate believed she was having a wild and raunchy fling with this brawny trucker.

She didn't care to dwell on why sexual subterfuge was suddenly so important to her. All she knew was that Nate had wounded her badly and she needed to retaliate. Unfortunately, he probably didn't give a flying flip who she slept with, but if there was one chance in a million she could make Nate Hawksmoor wince with jealousy—even for a second—she'd grab it!

NATE SLAMMED INTO his apartment and was rewarded for his show of temper by Trisha's frightened cry. He cast a repentant glance toward the couch where she'd been quietly lying in her carrier, playing with her fingers.

"Hell." He tossed the mail onto the coffee table

and bent over his squalling daughter. "I'm sorry, Tee." He unfastened the safety belt and picked her up, cuddling her against his chest. Pacing, he gingerly patted her back, trying to reassure her with soft murmurs.

"Daddy's sorry he slammed the door." He eyed the offending portal with umbrage. "Daddy's mad at himself. Daddy was a jerk and now Daddy's paying for it." He canted his head so he could better see Trisha's face. Her crying was coming in fits and spurts; he sensed she was calming down.

"That's better." He patted and pivoted around, scowling at the door. "It's almost time for lunch. We'll go in the kitchen, eat, and forget all about that laughing hyena and what hot things he and Hallie are doing to each other across the hall." He visualized Hallie, naked and desirable, moaning in her lover's arms. Biting off a curse, he closed his eyes.

Trisha hiccuped and let out a high-pitched whine.

"Yeah," he muttered. "I know the feeling." Crossing to the sofa, he sat down and lay Trisha on his thighs so he could look at her face. "Listen to me, young lady…" He held out a finger so she could grab it. "When you grow up…" He stopped, disconcerted. What did he want to tell her? "When you grow up…" he began again, then floundered once more.

He squinted at the apartment door, then down at his daughter who was now wide-eyed and staring at him. "Don't be pushy!" he finally said, but the advice didn't sit well. Why not? What did he want for his daughter? He'd never thought about it until this moment. Of course, a week ago he didn't even know he had a daughter, so it was all new to him—the responsibility as well as any hopes and dreams he might have for her. "Hopes and dreams?" he murmured. What were his hopes and dreams for little Trisha?

He scanned her face, those wide, innocent eyes, the sweet lips and the tiny cleft in her chin. Gently he stroked the almost nonexistent blond hair. "What do I want for you, Tee?" he asked softly.

She smiled and hiccuped.

He grinned at her, lifting the finger she held so tightly. Offering his other hand, she grabbed his index finger. He lifted, and she stuck like glue.

Something inside him, a place he'd never known existed, filled up with sunshine. Good God, he loved this little person. And damn it, he *did* have hopes and dreams for her. He didn't want his little girl to end up under any horny bastard's thumb. That realization made him sit up. He eyed his apartment door with a mixture of anger and regret. If Hallie had been his daughter, he'd have punched *himself* in the gut for what he did to her this morning. He was truly worse than a pig. He was the stuff slime wiped off its shoes.

He wanted better than that for Trisha. He didn't want her consorting with slime. He wanted some nice man to come along and love her, do things for her just because he cared.

His gut clenching, he gazed down at his baby daughter, recalling Hallie's scent and memories of roses and cut grass. "The Richmonds," he whispered. "I wonder if they had what it seemed like they had."

Trisha gurgled and smiled, drawing his gaze. He bent and kissed the chubby fingers desperately clutching his hand. "If they didn't, if there isn't such a thing, Tee, you have my permission to be exactly like

Miss Pushy across the hall.'' Unable to believe he'd uttered those words, he shook his head at himself. ''In an imperfect world, I'd rather you be a bully than be bullied.'' Bending lower, he whispered. ''This is our secret, okay?''

Trisha let go of his finger and grabbed his nose.

THAT EVENING Nate had a dinner date with Buffy. No matter what secret promises he'd made to Trisha, Buffy was still the type of woman he wanted. Nate himself had no intention of getting involved with a pushy woman. That's why it came as a shock to him that, even with Buffy's eye-grabbing cleavage and her ''Yes, my liege'' attitude, he was bored.

Telling her he had an early breakfast meeting with a client, he got rid of her by ten o'clock. When he arrived back at the apartment building, and passed by Hallie's door, he berated himself. Why in blazes had he shoved away a perfectly obliging woman because a few wires in his brain had gotten fouled over the holidays? Some peculiar short circuit was making him fantasize about Hallie St. John.

He came to a halt and glowered at her door. Just because he'd decided that Trisha might be better off if she was more like Hallie didn't mean *he* would be better off with a woman like her. He would not be dominated. No way, no how. Resolve solidifying in his belly, he shoved his key in the door before remembering that Trisha was upstairs with Goldie.

Irritated by his damaged concentration, he stalked back to the staircase and bounded upstairs two steps at a time. He started to get a bad feeling the instant he saw the yellow piece of paper taped to Goldie's door. He read the note, ground his teeth, and read it again, hoping the message would magically change. No. It still read, "Nate, dear boy, I've had a slight perfume accident and had to scurry to the emergency room. That nice Hallie downstairs said she'd keep Trisha while I'm gone. If you're reading this note, I'm still gone and Trisha is downstairs." It was signed, "Goldie."

"A slight perfume accident?" he muttered, wadding the note. That could mean anything from a cut finger to an noxious reaction to garlic fumes. Well, whatever it was, Goldie had been well enough to make sure Trisha was safe.

He sprang down the stairs, experiencing an unwanted sense of elation at the thought of seeing Hallie, though he didn't hold out much hope she would feel the same way. No doubt she would be put out that she'd been compelled to care for his baby, again.

Besides, he reminded himself grimly, Sugar would be there. He hoped the couple could restrain themselves from doing anything "hot" in front of the baby. He didn't relish the idea of his innocent child needing therapy. Neither did he relish the idea of interrupting Hallie and her hulking lover—witnessing their flushed faces, watching the tucking in of shirttails and the finger-combing of passionately mussed hair, or hearing lusty breathlessness in their voices.

With hearty misgivings, he knocked.

The door came open and Hallie stood there in a white sweater and green slacks, looking neither flushed nor mussed. The smile on her face faded, not doing much for his mood. "Oh, I thought it was— You're back early," she said.

He glanced over her shoulder to see Sugar sprawled in the middle of her living room floor, cooing and chattering to Trisha. His daughter lay on a pink baby blanket, hands and feet wagging in the air. Nate exhaled, surprised at how tense he'd been, harboring lewd visions of nude acrobatics. Looking back at Hallie, he smiled. He wasn't really happy, but he was certainly feeling better than before she'd opened the door. "I'm sorry about this. How's Goldie?"

Hallie stepped backward, allowing him to come in. "I don't know. She had her hand wrapped in a towel and jabbered too quickly for me to make much out of what happened. She mentioned she had a cab waiting and asked if I'd watch Trisha while she was at the hospital." Hallie shrugged. "I said yes and she vanished. That was twenty minutes ago."

Nate exhaled, frustrated. "I'm sorry to impose."

She lifted her hands as if to say it wasn't his fault. "Trisha's fine." Indicating the living room, she added, "Sugar's great with kids."

"Why not, he practically *is* one," Nate muttered, then cursed himself. What a lousy thing to say. Just because he had a case of creeping, crawling, green-eyed jealousy didn't give him any right to bad-mouth the big moose in front of Hallie.

She eyed Nate with displeasure. "You're in a fine mood. Rash chafing?"

He felt worse than awful. The emotional seesawing that had nagged him all day was taking a toll. Without thought, he took Hallie's hand and pulled her into a hidden corner away from the living room. "Look, Hallie, I'm sorry about this morning. I was a jerk to treat you the way I did." With a heaviness in his chest, he searched her eyes. They glimmered with hurt. "I'm a bastard. I know it and I'm not proud of it. But I think you understand what happened last night was something neither of us planned—and neither of us wanted..."

She swallowed visibly and blinked. He could tell she was fighting tears. "You're a beautiful, strong woman, Hallie," he whispered. "And you're sexy as hell, but you and I want different things. We both know it. I guess in my own clumsy way I was trying to make it easy for you to..." He shrugged, shaking his head. He wasn't a man to be at a loss for words, but he couldn't say it.

"To see how wrong we are for each other?"

He met her solemn gaze and nodded. "Yeah."

She looked away for a moment and sucked in a long, shuddery breath. When she faced him again, she smiled, though her eyes shimmered with melancholy. "In your own clumsy way, Nate, you did the right thing." She tugged her hand from his grasp. "I accept your apology." Turning her back on him, she rounded the corner into the living room.

He was surprised how little his apology helped. He still felt like punching something. It was as though all pleasure had deserted him, left him empty. He watched her walk away, and then remembered he was there for a reason that had nothing to do with how big a bastard he was. Pulling himself together, he followed her into the living room.

He glanced at Sugar who was holding a snow globe over Trisha's head, shaking it. The baby gurgled and clapped with delight. Despite his mood, the sight of his baby's bubbly grin made Nate smile. She was so pure, so devoid of spite and jealousy, of suspicion or lust. He wished he could freeze time, leave her in this blissful state of naiveté, never to know hurt or yearning or envy or guilt.

He squatted beside her and glanced again at the snow globe Sugar was shaking. He squinted in confusion. What the hell? He bent lower for a better look and was aghast. Inside the globe, what he'd thought was a snowman turned out to be a snow woman— complete with large, flesh-colored breasts.

Hallie knelt nearby, replacing toys in Trisha's diaper bag. Nate snagged her gaze and gave her a look, indicating the snow globe with a jerk of his head.

Her lips quirked. "Sugar's latest gift."

The trucker glanced up and grinned. "Oh, howdy, ol' buddy. Didn't hear you come in." He held out the globe so Nate could get a better view. Fake snow swirled around the obscene figure, which wore a frilly red apron and held a broom. "Ain't she a hoot?" he said. "Found her at a truck stop just outside Houston."

Nate eyed the globe with distaste. "Leaving her there didn't occur to you?" It was strange how Nate looked at things differently now that he had a baby to consider. He'd never thought of himself as a spoilsport, but this—this…this Frosty the Snow Hooker was being dangled in front of his innocent daughter's face!

Sugar laughed. "Trisha loves it. I was thinkin' Hallie might let me give it to her."

Nate peered at Hallie, frowning a warning.

"Uh, I don't think it's appropriate for a baby," Hallie said, no doubt reading Nate's glare loud and clear. "But it's a sweet thought, Sugar."

The trucker's brow puckered. "Huh?" He glanced at the snow woman for a minute, seeming to ponder Hallie's remark, then grinned sheepishly. "Oh. Right. Sure. I get it." He nodded, enclosing the offending globe in a big paw. "I'll bring her something else next time I come through. There's these great rubber snakes."

Nate gathered up his daughter.

"Sorry, ol' buddy." Sugar sat back, prudently placing the globe behind him. "I guess I wasn't thinking."

Nate glanced at the man, fighting an urge to say, "So, what's new?" Instead, he smiled. "It's not necessary to get Trisha anything."

"Shucks, it's a pleasure. I love kids and I don't have any family."

Hallie touched Sugar's shoulder with obvious affection and Nate experienced a stab of jealousy. "I bet Trisha would love a teddy bear, Sugar."

The trucker snapped beefy fingers. "Hell! Why didn't I think of that?"

Nate held his tongue, though the idea that Sugar wasn't well acquainted with the concept of thinking flitted across his mind again. When he stood, Hallie rose, too, hoisting the diaper bag. She indicated the door. "Trisha's had her bottle and I just changed her." Walking with him to the door, she handed him the bag. "I bet if you put her to bed, she'll go right to sleep."

He scanned Hallie's unsmiling face, feeling awkward, something he hadn't felt around a woman since he was twelve. "Thanks."

"No problem." She ran a hand through her bangs, brushing them out of her eyes. "I don't turn babies in need away from my door."

He grinned at her. "I know." *How inane!*

Her gaze darted away and he was sorry she broke

eye contact. "Hallie," he ventured, not sure what the hell he planned to say.

She glanced his way, but focused on his chin. He bent his knees, snagging her gaze. "Thanks," he repeated, feeling acutely stupid. *Is that all you can say to the woman, idiot?*

"Hallie, darlin'," Sugar called. "I think I'll go take a shower."

She waved him off. "Okay." When she turned back to Nate, she presented him with a pinched expression. "You thanked me already." Crossing her arms, she shifted from foot to foot. He sensed she was restless, anxious for him to leave. "You're welcome?" Her expression was confused. "Is that what you're waiting for?"

He leaned against her door, cuddling Trisha in one arm, the heavy bag clasped in the other. "No." Bending forward, he kissed her cheek, dismayed with himself. Why the hell had he done that? It had only been a kiss on the cheek. A brotherly thing. But he sure as hell didn't feel brotherly. All he knew was that in a few minutes she'd be slipping naked into a shower with Sugar, the incredible, hulking, good ol' boy. Considering how rotten that made him feel, Hallie was lucky his hands were full or he might have embarrassed them both.

She blinked, staring. She was so cute when she was in shock. After a second, she lifted her chin, a sure indication she was coming out of it. "What was that, your clumsy way of telling me?" she rasped.

"That I..." He shook his head. He had no idea. At least nothing he could put his finger on. "Good night?"

Grimacing, she nudged him away from the door.

Turning the knob, she emphasized her desire for him to leave. "In the future, just go," she muttered. "I'll get the idea."

THE NEXT AFTERNOON around two o'clock, Nate and Trisha returned to the apartment from a brisk walk to the supermarket. Trisha was strapped to his back and looked like the cutest little Eskimo inside or outside Alaska. Nate lugged two heavy bags of groceries, muttering that the first thing after the holidays he was definitely buying a new car—one that Trisha could ride in.

He was hell-bent on not asking Hallie for any more help, and between his daughter's need for bulky boxes of diapers and cans of formula, and his own need for foodstuffs, he'd either die of exhaustion trekking back and forth to the grocery store, a mile away, or he'd be Mr. Universe before spring.

He settled his bags in the hallway in front of his apartment door and fished for his key. A low moan from across the hall caught his attention. He stilled, listening against his will.

It came again. A low, masculine moan. He shifted to stare at the door, swallowing bile. Did they have to play their sex games right inside the door?

Nate heard feminine laugher and his blood ran cold.

"Oh, Sugar, how can you bend that way? You must be double-jointed!"

Sugar's moan became a deep, suggestive chuckle.

"Hell." Nate rubbed his eyelids, attempting to erase the perverted images crowding his brain. "I'm in hell."

9

NATE BROKE OUT in a sweat that had nothing to do with the fact that he was wearing a parka and a baby. He eyed Hallie's door with frustration.

"Don't do that, Sugar," Hallie cried, giggling. "We'll get stuck this way."

"I can do it," Sugar insisted.

An unwelcome surge of possessiveness washed over Nate. "*Don't,* damn it!" he muttered, his eyes squeezed tight as he tried not to visualize what he was visualizing.

"Ooo-ooh!" Hallie sounded as if she was in pain. That rat was forcing her into positions that were unhealthy.

Sugar groaned. "I can't hold it much longer."

"What's going on?"

Nate jumped at the sound of Goldie's squawky question. Apparently she'd been able to hear the moaning and laughing and groaning upstairs. Nate's eyes snapped open and he realized he'd moved closer to Hallie's door.

"Do you think they're hurt?" Goldie asked, her chipmunk-like features pinched with worry.

Nate shook himself, trying to return to solid mental ground. He focused on Goldie. Her short frizzy hair was the color of ripe persimmons. Nate wondered how she managed to get her lips the same exact shade. And why.

Goldie squinted fretfully at the door, then at Nate when Hallie cried out again. "I think they're sick," Goldie whined. Without waiting for Nate to object, she pounded on Hallie's door. Nate stood there as if paralyzed, not wanting to see what he knew he'd see—Hallie's face, bright with the glow of interrupted sex, as she peeked out from behind a crack in the door.

He dropped his gaze only to find himself looking at Goldie's jeans-clad buttocks. He marveled at how she wedged her ample derriere into those tight pants. He didn't know how she breathed. Goldie was obviously proud of her bounteous figure. In her day-to-day costume of jeans, boots, and bright flannel shirts, she looked like the lead character in some offbeat play titled *Tweedle-Dum Does Dallas,* or in Goldie's case, *Tulsa.*

She knocked again, shouting, "Is everybody okay in there?"

"Look, Goldie..." Nate flinched at how raspy his voice sounded. "They're fine."

The older woman aimed reproachful gray eyes his way. "They can't be! I swear I heard somebody scream out."

Nate eyed heaven. Evidently neither Goldie nor the late Mr. Feldick had ever felt the urge to scream during sex.

A rattling noise told Nate that Hallie's door was opening. He stiffened, feeling as if he'd been caught with his hand in her underwear drawer. And blast if he knew why he should feel guilty about standing outside his own apartment. He hadn't done a thing but come home from the supermarket.

Hallie appeared, smoothing her sweater into place. Nate felt heat rush up his neck, his worst fears realized. "Yes?"

"Are you all right, dear?" Goldie cried. "From upstairs I heard moaning, and when I got down here, Nate was listening at your door, so I know he was concerned, too."

With Goldie's damning remark, Nate's breathing shut down. His gaze shot to Hallie's. He knew his expression was as guilty as sin, and wondered why.

"We thought we'd better investigate," Goldie hurried on to explain, unaware that she'd made Nate out to be the neighborhood pervert. "Is there anything we can do?"

Hallie's lips parted as she stared at him. When Goldie finished her rambling, Hallie dragged her gaze to the older woman. "We're fine, thanks." She peered at Nate once more.

"Are you sure there's nothing we can do?" Goldie persisted, and Nate wondered if in another incarnation the woman had been a bulldog. "What about your gentleman friend? He seemed to be doing most of the groaning."

Nate winced. If he recalled correctly—which he did—Hallie could make a man groan. *A lot*. He felt his gut tighten as erotic memories flooded back.

The door creaked and he realized Hallie was opening it fully. She indicated behind her. "He's okay." She called. "Aren't you, Sugar?"

Nate stared at the sight in front of him. A big plastic game mat had been laid out on the carpet. The mat held four rows of colored circles, each row a different color. Sugar was standing on the mat. Well, sort of standing. He was actually contorted like a pretzel, legs crossed, body arched backward, right hand planted painfully close to his left foot. He looked like a sculpture that might have been entitled simply *Ouch!*

"I'm gonna fall," Sugar called with a laugh.

"Go ahead," Hallie said. "I'm giving you this round."

Goldie's giggle sounded like a cross between a crow's caw and hiccups. "You young people, today. What you won't do for fun."

Nate felt as if a stone had dissolved inside him. Slowly, humor germinated and grew. What a stupid ass he was! What wild, perverse things he'd been thinking, eating himself up with jealousy. And all they were doing was playing Milton Bradley's Twister. Relief washed over him even as he reminded himself that, hot sex or not, it wasn't his business. Hallie's love life and the games she played with her lovers were of no interest to him.

He grinned, his mood suddenly light. He wasn't aware he'd chuckled out loud until Hallie turned to glare at him. His laughter died.

"Well…" He cleared his throat. "I'd better get these groceries inside."

"Nate, dear. One second," Goldie said. "I was wondering if you three young people would like to come up and have dinner with me tonight." She held up her left hand. The middle finger was bandaged and stood obscenely erect. "I have all the makings of lasagna, but I'm not used to this bulky bandage, yet, so I'm having a little trouble in the kitchen." She faced him. "Your darling baby girl is welcome, naturally."

She smiled at him and then Hallie. "Please, come. And afterward I have a thank-you surprise for you all."

Hallie's grin was polite and tentative at best. Nate watched, anticipating her no. Sugar thudded to a heap on the Twister mat. "I love lasagna," he shouted. "We'll bring salad, won't we, Hallie, darlin'?"

Holding her strained smile in place, Hallie nodded. "Sure. Okay." Nate could tell she wasn't thrilled to be having dinner with Nate the Pervert. Unfortunately for him, he couldn't turn down Goldie's invitation. He owed the woman for baby-sitting. Helping with dinner was little enough to do.

"What time?" Hallie asked.

"Let's make it early, say four-thirty? We have to put the lasagna together first, and it takes a while to cook." She looked at Nate. "What do you say?"

He winked. "Can't wait."

Goldie clapped her hands the best she could. "Great. This way we can have a good long visit." She tweaked Nate's cheek. "Now aren't you glad we checked on them rather than just listening at the door, silly boy? Everything's okay. Just like I thought!" She patted his face, unaware that Hallie was glaring openly at him now.

He smiled at Goldie, though it was an effort. "Right."

Heading toward the stairs, Goldie waved over her shoulder. "See you in two hours, kids."

Nate's glance swerved back to Hallie. Behind her, Sugar was nowhere in sight, and neither was the Twister mat. Hallie startled Nate by stepping outside her apartment and closing the door. Leaning against it, she eyed him uncertainly. "What were you doing listening at my door?"

Trisha took that opportunity to whimper. His daughter had wonderful timing, bless her little heart. Shifting, he indicated the baby strapped to his back. "I'd better get her out of that snowsuit before she melts."

Hallie's expression darkened, but he knew she would never detain him if Trisha's well-being was at stake.

He turned away, but an inner voice nagged that he was being a sniveling chicken. The last thing he wanted to believe about himself was that he was a coward—afraid to tell a woman the simple truth. He was in control of his life, and by damn, he had nothing to feel guilty about.

He turned back. "Look, I was *not* listening at your door," he said grimly. "Trisha and I got home with groceries and I heard a moan. I turned around. It's only natural." He shrugged. "Goldie came down right then and jumped to the worst possible conclusion." Hallie's expression was damning, making him feel as if he should at least be offered a last cigarette before she shouted, "Ready. Aim. Fire!" "I may be a bastard, Hallie, but I'm not a sick bastard."

Her expression didn't change, but after a minute she gestured toward his door. "Go. Take care of Trisha."

He eyed her gravely. "You think I'm a pervert?"

She felt around for her doorknob. "No," she said quietly. "I believe you." A second later she was gone.

Nate unlocked his door, puzzled. He'd watched her

eyes when she'd said she believed him, and he knew she'd told the truth.

So why didn't he get the sense she was relieved?

AT PRECISELY four-thirty, Nate left his apartment, holding a sleeping Trisha in her carrier. He'd just locked his door when Hallie emerged from her apartment carrying a big bowl of salad.

She acknowledged him stiffly, her demeanor cool and wary.

He nodded. "Where's Wayne?" He hoped she would believe his interest purely conversational. He wished it was.

"Sugar'll be along. He took a nap and overslept, so he's changing."

Nate opted not to ask why she hadn't simply rolled over and nudged him awake. However, her sex life wasn't of any interest to him, so he kept his troubling preoccupation with the subject to himself.

Hallie smiled at Trisha and Nate felt a curious warming at the sight. When their eyes met, he smiled, too, unable to do otherwise.

"She's so sweet," Hallie whispered, sounding wistful.

Nate glanced at his daughter, who was freshly bathed and dressed in a pink sleeper. She did look like an angel, if he said so himself. She'd been cranky that afternoon, so he'd fed her a little early and she'd dropped right off. "I bet she wakes up at ten and wants to party all night," he said.

Hallie's laughter was soft and sweet. "As soon as we get dinner on, we can wake her and play with her. If we're lucky we'll tire her out and she'll sleep through the night."

"Good plan." Nate liked her use of "we." It seemed natural, somehow. Maybe it was because he'd done almost nothing with his daughter that hadn't involved Hallie. But as it had been virtually every other time, this was *her* plan. Shades of his mother. His mood took a nosedive. When he noticed Hallie's smile fade, he realized his thoughts must have shown on his face.

Confirming that she'd read his thoughts, Hallie whirled around and marched toward the stairs. "Kill me for having an opinion," she muttered.

Nate exhaled slowly, shaking his head. He hadn't even said a word and she'd flown off the handle. She disappeared, but he could hear her brisk footfalls as she dashed up the steps. "Damn woman's too pushy and too touchy," he muttered.

Then why are you so damn hot for her, Hawksmoor?

GOLDIE'S APARTMENT was the same floor plan as Hallie's, but any similarity beyond that was undetectable. Along with Ferdie Feldick the First, and little Ferdie, Goldie had moved into that third-floor apartment in the early seventies. She obviously still had the original carpeting—vintage celery shag. Her walls were painted a matching shade of green, where there was any wall to see. Goldie had covered nearly every inch from ceiling to floor with framed photographs of her family or cherished drawings by the grandchildren.

Shiny knickknack shelves and glass-fronted cabinets dotted the walls between the hodgepodge of frames. These haphazardly arranged curio shelves were crammed with her collection of cherubic figurines, along with hundreds of miniature ceramic fish, fowl, and cutsie four-legged critters.

Her sofa and easy chairs, also celery-green, were as pristine as whatever day in the nineteen seventies they were purchased, because they had been preserved beneath clear vinyl slipcovers. There wasn't a speck of dust in the place. Goldie's shag carpet stood at stately attention, rake marks in excessive evidence all over the floor. Hallie felt like a mugger every time she took a step.

The place reeked with the pungent tang of Goldie's perfume experiments, but there was no sign of them in the living room or kitchen. Evidently she, too, used her second bedroom as her office. Or in Goldie's case, her lab.

The apartments on Hallie's side of the building were smaller than those on Nate's, and didn't have fireplaces. So, leave it to Goldie to have a video of a crackling log fire. All evening Goldie played and replayed the fake inferno on her little portable set. More than once Hallie had the urge to jump up and yell, "Your TV's on fire!" but caught herself in the nick of time.

Dinner was enjoyable, in spite of the fact that Hallie had to sit across from Nate and was unable to avoid meeting his gaze. She tried desperately to focus on Goldie, chattering away about the grandkids or her beloved, perfect son, Ferdie. Hallie fought a grin as Goldie talked on and on about Ferdie's flourishing fertilizer firm.

Hallie caught Nate running a hand across his mouth, hiding his own mirth at the comical overuse of words beginning with *F*. Their eyes met for an instant, his sparkling with laughter. It was a nice instant sharing a secret joke. But it was over quickly and they avoided looking at each other again. That saddened Hallie, and she knew she was stupid to let it.

Everything about Nate saddened Hallie, ever since…that night. She didn't want to think about how sad things suddenly were, but her heart refused to lighten no matter how hard she worked at it. Even with the amiable Sugar hanging around to make jokes and keep her occupied with mindless games, she felt weighted down by gloom.

Why did she have to be attracted to Nate? Why did she crave his touch, pine for his kisses? Maybe it was true that women were attracted to the familiar. That was why women with alcoholic fathers so often chose alcoholic mates, and women of abusive fathers chose abusers.

Hallie had thought, since she *knew* how destructive controlling men could be, she'd never fall for one. She knew all too well not to fall into the trap of loving a man who ruled with an iron hand.

Didn't she?

Just because Nate was gentle and giving in bed, that was no reason to let herself get screwed up on the subject of dominant men. He was wrong for her. He wanted a wimp-woman. And as sure as the sun came up every morning, if she let her heart get tangled with his, he'd try to turn her into one. *No! No! No!*

''No?'' Goldie demanded, wrenching Hallie from her worrisome musings. Embarrassed that she had no idea what they'd been talking about, she scanned Goldie's face for some clue. The older woman glowered at her as though she'd said no she didn't care to breathe any longer, thank you.

"You didn't like the dinner?"

Hallie's cheeks burned. "Uh, of course I did. It was delicious."

Goldie hunched forward, not a good sign. "Well, then, what were you saying no for?"

Hallie knew her face was flaming and it was very possible her ears were smoking. From beneath her lashes, she chanced a peek at Nate. He watched her, his expression unreadable. "Uh..." She cleared her throat. "I said, 'Go.'" She made a bleak attempt at a grin. "Go, girl! Great meal." She made a thumbs-up signal, feeling about as foolish as she ever intended to feel.

"But you said it three times, dear," Goldie persisted. "'No! No! No!' is what you said."

Hallie wanted to slide from her chair and belly-crawl out the door. But she was afraid they might notice. Trying to be brave, she labored to keep smiling, lifting her fisted thumbs-up higher. "I, uh, said, Go! Go! Go!" She was afraid now her smile looked more like a pained squint. She bit her lip, wishing she weren't such a pathetic liar.

"Right on!" Sugar struck the same thumbs-up pose. "Go! Go! Go! My compliments to us. Right, Nate, ol' buddy?"

Against her better judgment, Hallie's glance met Nate's. Slowly, deliberately, he lifted his water glass, his gaze trained on her. "Go, go, go!"

From his wry tone, Hallie could tell he was taunting her. The man *knew* she'd blurted, "No," not "Go." She prayed he wasn't perceptive enough to sense who she'd been thinking about, or what she'd been denying.

Thirty minutes later Hallie put away the last dinner dish she'd been drying when Goldie tapped her on the shoulder. "Here you are, dear. Merry Christmas." The older woman held out a small gift-wrapped package, about the size that might contain a perfume bottle. With trepidation, Hallie accepted it. "Oh, Goldie, you shouldn't have," she said, appalled that she had. "I don't have a thing for you."

The older woman patted Hallie's arm. "Silly thing, I *want* to!" Her expression full of expectancy, she cried, "Open it."

Hallie obliged and was not surprised to find a bottle containing a purple, hand-drawn label. "'Goldie's Nose Posies,'" she read out loud, then glanced up. "Nice name."

Goldie's smile broadened. "That's the name of my company, once I go public. This is my newest fragrance, Lilies of Lasagna." She laughed as though at some private joke. "Tonight you ate it, now you can wear it!" Plucking the bottle from Hallie's fingers, Goldie pointed it at her and sprayed.

Hallie barely had time to shut her eyes before the funky fog hit her in the face. Trying to suppress a cough, she almost blew out her eardrums. "How—unique..." she murmured. It smelled vaguely like lasagna—candied lasagna. She wished she hadn't been subjected to such a big dose on a full stomach. "Thank you," she said, trying to mean it.

"It's my pleasure, dear girl." Taking Hallie's hand, she led her into the living room where the men sat on opposite ends of the sofa, wrapped gifts in their hands. Little Trisha was in her carrier between them, sound asleep after the playtime they had put her through before dinner. "Well, men?" Goldie said with a meaningful lift of her brows. "Aren't you going to open your presents?"

"We were waiting for you," Nate said, lifting the small box and removing the ribbon. Able to breathe again without fear of choking to death, Hallie watched with watery eyes, wondering if they, too, got Lilies of Lasagna.

Sugar was the first to rip his open. He stared at the bottle, looking baffled.

"It's aftershave," Goldie said. "It sprays. Spray some on."

Nate had his open now. Hallie watched his lips quirk. "'Hamburger After Midnight.'"

"I thought that 'after midnight' part made it sound sexy." Goldie rushed to him and snatched the bottle. She sprayed him enthusiastically, just as she'd sprayed Hallie, but she hit him in the neck, so at least his vision was spared.

"Thanks, Goldie." He inhaled and grinned. "It smells just like a hamburger heavy on the onions."

Sugar sprayed himself in the chest. "Shoot, I've never smelled like a hamburger before." He grinned at Goldie. "Great idea. I've always wondered why those pretty-boy designers thought real men wanted to smell like tree bark or some gas spewed out by a horny billy goat."

Nate burst out laughing and Hallie caught her breath at the beauty of the sparkle in his eyes. "Good point," he said. The others joined in the merriment— even Hallie, who couldn't help being affected by Nate's easy smile and rich laughter.

"Next time I come to town, Goldie," Sugar said, "I'll bring you back somethin'."

Hallie and Nate exchanged amused glances, and it surprised Hallie that they did it so naturally, immediately knowing how the other felt. Her amusement faded at that realization. She didn't need to be sharing secret jokes with this guy. She didn't want to share *anything* with him.

"Instead of buying me a present, Sugar, I'll tell you what you can do for me," Goldie said. "And it won't cost you a nickel."

The three looked at her. Uneasiness crept up Hallie's spine. She had no idea what to expect of this eccentric woman.

"Name it, Goldie." Sugar slapped his knee. Hallie gaped at him in wonder. Didn't the man *ever* think? What if she asked them to take cartons of her homemade Nose Posies and sell it door to door?

"I'm holding you to that, dear." Goldie beamed at Sugar. "Go get that game you were playing with Hallie this afternoon and let's all have a go. It looked like fun."

Sugar guffawed and lumbered to his feet. "You got a deal, Goldie." He fished in his pocket and pulled out his key to Hallie's place. "Be right back."

Hallie took in the goings-on with a sense of unreality. The four of them weren't really going to play Twister, were they? What if by some ghastly fluke she got tangled up with Nate!

She shot him a glance. He lounged on the sofa, an arm draped across the back. When their eyes met, his lips twisted wryly. The unruly twinkle in his eyes made Hallie nervous.

10

THE THOUGHT of getting her body tangled up with Nate's—again—brought on sheer panic.

"But Goldie," she blurted, desperately searching for a plausible excuse not to play. "I, well...what about your finger?" She experienced a wave of relief. *Yes!* "You wouldn't want to do more damage to your poor finger."

Goldie looked at her bandaged middle finger, then back at Hallie. "Do I have to use it?"

"Well, not specifically." Hallie wished the game rules included fingertip push-ups. "But you'll have to put your hands on the mat and bear some of your weight with them. It probably wouldn't be wise to risk it."

Goldie waved the idea off as if she was swatting a gnat. "Not a problem, dear." She bent forward, planted the flats of her hands on the carpet and pushed up with her feet. To Hallie's astonishment, Goldie did a perfect handstand. "My family was all circus folk. Before I married Ferdie the First, I was part of the Tumbling Tugwaddles." Goldie dropped her booted feet to the floor and straightened. "Didn't hurt my finger a bit, see?" Grinning broadly, she held up the bandaged appendage.

Nate's low chuckle drew Hallie's glance. "That settles it, I want Goldie to be my partner."

"I'm flattered, dear boy." She hugged his neck. "I'll make you proud."

Nate winked at her, then eyed Hallie. "I hope for your sake, you're flexible, Miss St. John."

Agitated and flustered, Hallie swept her hand up to shove back her bangs. She made a point of avoiding Nate's gaze. He knew exactly how flexible she was!

Hot recollections making her knees weak, Hallie sank into a plastic-covered easy chair. Well, at least she wouldn't be playing with Nate. That was a load off her mind.

The apartment door burst open. Sugar reappeared, the game under his arm. "Okay, guys and gals, let's get this show on the road. Who wants to go first?"

"I'm game." Nate got up from the couch. "Goldie and I are a team."

"Okay," Sugar said. "Then Nate and Hallie go first."

Before Hallie realized what was happening Nate stood before her. "Come on, little Miss Adversary." He offered her his hand.

Hallie blanched. What was going on here? She thought Nate would be tangling himself up with Goldie! "But—but, you're on Goldie's team."

Nate wagged his fingers as if to suggest she was stalling. "I am. You don't play against your own partner, sweetheart. I thought you knew the rules."

With a sinking feeling in her stomach, she realized he was right. Where was her mind? "Well..." She struggled to find an excuse not to get on that mat with him. "W-why don't you play with Sugar?"

Nate grinned. "That's not how the game is played. At least not when I play it."

"Nope," Sugar put in. "It's boy-girl, boy-girl,

Hallie, darlin'," Sugar said as he and Goldie smoothed out the mat.

"It's just a game," Nate murmured. "Truce?"

She eyed his outstretched hand with mistrust, then glared at him. He'd known exactly what he was doing when he asked Goldie to be his partner!

He wasn't grinning now, but those dratted eyes smiled at her. Warmly. Against her will and her better judgment, she found herself accepting his hand. Struggling with all her might, she managed to hold on to her withering stare. "As long as you understand I don't *like* you, Mr. Hawksmoor," she murmured under her breath.

It wasn't exactly a lie—it was her most *urgent desire* not to like him. As soon as Hallie was standing, she pulled her hand from Nate's. Still groping for excuses not to play with him, she blurted, "I think we should all play together. You can play with four people."

Goldie finished smoothing out the four- by-six-foot mat and straightened as Sugar scooped up the spinner. "It's too hard to spin with us all playing. Remember how hard it was this afternoon?" He plopped down on the carpet. "Me and Goldie'll spin for you two. Whoever stays out there for the most spins without falling wins for their team."

Goldie sat down next to Sugar and stretched her pudgy legs out in front of her. The older woman grabbed her toes and pulled her nose to her knees. Hallie stared, aghast. The ex-Tumbling Tugwaddle was as flexible as a rubber band.

"Sounds like a plan," Nate said, drawing Hallie's dismayed gaze. He grinned at her, then whispered in an aside, "Don't throw this thing by falling on purpose. Remember, I've seen you in action."

She frowned with contempt, her cheeks blazing. "Don't you worry," she assured him, "I'll stay up longer than you do, even if I end up in traction."

He winked. "I doubt it, sweetheart, but you're welcome to try."

The gall of the man, goading her with a cheeky wink! The idea of their body parts being tangled together scared her silly, but she'd be damned before she'd let him win. Not now! And *after* she beat him, he'd be too whipped to wink, the egotistical jerk!

The game began with Hallie and Nate on opposite sides of the mat. But soon, Hallie was ducking beneath him, her head below his. She looked at Goldie, waiting for her to spin. Nate's breath in her ear was quite disturbing. "Hi," he whispered, his voice tinged with amusement. "Haven't we been here before?"

"Shush," she hissed. "It's your turn. Goldie said, 'Right foot in yellow.'" She made the mistake of glancing at him.

He gave her a slow smile. "Okay. Hold still."

"Hold still?" she echoed.

She gasped as he fit his thigh snugly between her legs, flush up against the center seam of her jeans. At the intimate contact, she almost toppled over in shock, but luckily got herself under control in time. She eyed the row of yellow dots. He'd chosen the least convenient one. There were two nearer him that were perfectly free, the conniving bum.

"You think you're funny?" she whispered hoarsely.

He grinned, his lips so close she could almost taste them. "Your turn."

She began to regret her rash pledge that she wouldn't give up until she needed traction. She was a fool for letting Nate provoke her into this stupid challenge. Sugar would never have manipulated her that way. Why couldn't the snug fit of the trucker's thigh wedged between her legs make her want to lick and moan and claw and purr the way Nate's solid, warm...

"You're not moving," Nate observed, startling her.

Hallie hadn't heard Sugar's instructions. "What?" she squeaked. "Repeat that?"

Sugar did and Hallie was able to move her leg so that Nate's leg was no longer between hers. She was now positioned solidly on all fours. She felt a little silly with her bottom thrust high in the air, like a hot-to-trot poodle looking for action. But at least she was no longer riding Nate's hard, provocative thigh.

Goldie called out Nate's move and to Hallie's dismay, it put his hips directly over her. The poodle, it seemed, had found some action. She bit her lip in mortification.

She could feel Nate in all the wrong places, from the curve of her ear where his hot breath tickled, to her bottom, crushed against what appeared to be a growing problem. She groaned, squeezing her eyes shut. It did no good. She felt every hard, sexy millimeter of him.

"Having a problem?" he asked.

"No!" she rasped in a whisper. "You're the one having the problem."

"It's an involuntary response. You're as much to blame as I am."

She went all sizzly and cold at the same time. Oh, Lord! She could feel the telltale pressure, exciting and troubling. "Oh—no..." The last thing she wanted was to be sexually stimulated by this man—and with an audience, yet!

"This has stopped being fun, Hallie," he murmured hoarsely. *"Give up."*

"You give up!"

"Damn it! You!"

"You!"

"Are you two fighting?" Goldie asked.

"No!" Hallie shouted, then tried to control her voice. "He just—I just..."

"She has the hiccups," Nate interjected.

"She does?" Goldie asked. "Well, that's no problem. The best way to get rid of hiccups is drinking water upside down. You're in the perfect position. I'll get a glass."

"No, Goldie," Hallie cried, "I don't—"

"No bother at all, dear." She pushed up from the carpet. "You two hold still. I'll be right back."

"Water sounds like an idea." Sugar hopped up to follow her. "On second thought, you got any cola?"

"Tons, dear boy." The two disappeared into the kitchen. The room became deadly still, but for the crackle of Goldie's fake TV fire.

Hallie's arms began to tremble. She hoped it was from fatigue because she didn't want to be reacting to Nate's—problem. "See what you did?" she snapped. "Thanks to you, I have to drink water upside down. I'll drown."

His wry chuckle tingled through her. "You don't want to have to tell them what we were talking about, do you?"

She thought about that for a minute. She certainly didn't. "Give up, Nate."

"Not likely, sweetheart."

She canted her head so she could scowl at his profile. "Well, don't count on me to do it!"

He grinned. "You're a pain, woman. I wish you didn't make me hot."

At his unexpected admission, her mouth sagged open and she could only stare.

"Why shouldn't I say it?" he asked. "I'm not hiding the fact very well."

She dropped her gaze to stare blankly at the mat. She felt as if her head was filling up with blood. Boiling blood. Her arms trembled so badly she was afraid he'd notice. Her heart was beating the rat-a-tat of a spring rain on window glass. Something warm touched her nape—lips pressed lightly in a kiss. She sucked in a shocked breath.

"I couldn't help it," he said.

"Well, control yourself, buster." She cast a glance toward the kitchen door. Goldie and Sugar were nowhere in sight. "Besides, a kiss is not involuntary!" Her arms vibrated like tuning forks. Her legs were as insubstantial as noodles. She was afraid in another few seconds she'd sag, face-first, to the mat.

"It wasn't a kiss in the strictest sense of the word."

"Oh, *really?*" she jeered. "Don't tell me it was a gag reflex!"

His low laughter was husky. "You smell like lasagna."

She felt something else, something she could only describe as a tongue stroking along the back of her neck. With an intense shiver, her limbs gave way and she collapsed.

"You don't *taste* like lasagna, though."

Scrambling around, she glared at him from flat on

her back. "You—*you!*" Reaching up, she grabbed fistfuls of his shirtfront. "You *licked* me!"

"I tasted you," he corrected.

"You *cheated!* Oof!" she tugged on his shirt.

Nate fell on top of her, though his arms continued to support enough of his weight so she wasn't crushed. "Look what you did," he taunted. "You made me fall, you bully."

"Rotten, manipulative cheat!" she cried, hating that she sounded breathless.

He grinned and her heartbeat skyrocketed. "You're pushy."

She sent frantic orders to her arms to shove him off. Unfortunately, disobedience ran rampant through her body parts. Her arms did nothing they were told to do. Her hands remained curled into fists, clutching wads of his shirt. To an unwitting observer, it might look as if she was actually dragging Nate *toward* her. His face did seem nearer, somehow. She sucked in an apprehensive breath. "You're not going to lick me again, are you!"

"Nope."

Before she had a chance to respond, his mouth covered hers, demanding gently, throwing her emotions into pandemonium. The intimacy of his kiss seemed so right, exactly the way it had the first time.

Suddenly, Hallie was overwhelmed by the unwelcome knowledge that was billowing inside her; a knowledge she had rejected and denied with all her strength.

She was in love with Nate Hawksmoor.

A suffocating sense of failure tightened her throat, even as she wholeheartedly kissed him back, quivering with the rapture and the tenderness of his kiss.

Even as her arms encircled his neck, and held him tightly, she was tormented by the evidence of her stupid, stupid weakness.

She cried out against his lips, but when the sound reached her ears, it was a lovesick moan. His mouth was so gentle, so persuasive. She hated herself for becoming lost in the thrill of it, but she was greedy for more.

Tears welled behind her eyelids as the last remnants of sanity slipped away, though it clawed and clutched for purchase. In silent desperation she clung to him, wanting the kiss to go on and on, longing to make wild, heathen love to him as they had on that one special, crazy night. Yet she was also praying with all her heart that this misconceived deed would end, that she could regain her good judgment, have the strength to run— *Run*—

"Well, well," Goldie said with a cawing titter. "Looks like Nate found a way to cure Hallie's hiccups."

"Yeah," Sugar said. "Maybe we oughta toss this glass of water on the both of 'em. Cool 'em down."

Hallie's eyes snapped wide open, and she found the will to push against Nate. He seemed to return to reality quickly, too, for an instant later he was off of her and sitting up.

It took Hallie longer to regain her poise. From her flat-on-the-back position, she ran both hands through her hair and peered guiltily at Goldie and Sugar.

"So, what did we miss?" Goldie asked, setting the water glass on the coffee table.

Avoiding eye contact with everybody, Hallie shakily came up on one elbow.

''We fell,'' Nate said, then cleared the hoarseness from his throat.

Hallie looked at him, but he didn't look at her. His jaw worked and he seemed put out. She averted her gaze, miffed. *He* was put out? Just who had started this whole thing anyway?

''You both fell?'' Sugar asked, taking his seat beside the spinner. ''At the same time?''

''Yeah,'' Nate said.

''Is that one of the rules?'' Goldie asked with enthusiasm. ''When you fall at the same time you kiss?''

''I think *they* invented that one.'' Sugar peered speculatively at Nate.

''Look, Wayne, I'm sorry about that,'' Nate muttered. Hallie could tell he was getting to his feet. ''It was my fault.''

Sugar opened his mouth to say something, but Goldie broke in. ''It's my Nose Posies! Right? You couldn't resist my Lilies of Lasagna!'' She tweaked Hallie's chin. ''Men love meat.'' She canted her head, scanning Hallie's face. Her grin dimmed. ''You look terribly flushed, dear. Maybe I need to water down my formula.''

''Maybe...'' Hallie nodded ruefully and crawled off the mat, wanting nothing more than to continue crawling away until she could lock herself in her bedroom and cry. How could fate be so fickle and vile as to make her fall in love with Nate Hawksmoor?

Sugar gave Hallie a nudge. ''I guess we'll have to break the tie. You guys ready to spin?''

She nodded numbly. As she settled on the rug, she chanced a peek at Nate. He stared at her, looking puzzled. Apparently he'd expected Sugar to punch his lights out. She shifted her gaze to Sugar. He lumbered into position to start the game. There wasn't a speck of jealous blood in his eye.

She sighed heavily. By now, Nate was probably having some major doubts that Sugar was her lover. Maybe she should have let the big guy in on the ruse.

Until this moment, Hallie hadn't realized how fiendish hindsight could sometimes be.

THE NEXT MORNING, Nate had the bad luck to open his door as Sugar was exiting Hallie's apartment. He was still uncomfortable about the kiss he'd inflicted on Hallie last night. He hadn't slept well, tossing and turning, mystified about what had come over him.

Sugar tipped his Stetson. "Morning, ol' buddy." He slung his canvas duffel over his shoulder. "Getting the paper?"

Nate nodded. "Yeah."

"Got ours already."

Ours! Nate felt terrible for having intruded into another man's territory. "Look, Wayne, about last night. I want to apologize again for that kiss. You and Hallie didn't have a problem about that, did you?"

Sugar's brows came down in a puckered frown. "Problem?"

Nate squatted to get his paper, wondering what it took to get something through this guy's head. Maybe a two-by-four. Maybe he shouldn't have brought it up. If Sugar was so thick he didn't register what another man kissing his lover might mean, then Nate didn't want to bring trouble down on Hallie's head by working his mouth when he shouldn't. Standing, he slapped the newspaper against his thigh, trying to look nonchalant. "Are you back on the road for a while?"

Sugar's perplexed frown eased. "Yep. Probably won't be back through T-Town for weeks." He bobbed his head. "But don't you worry. I'll sure bring your little girl that teddy bear next time I'm through."

Nate winced. He'd kissed Sugar's girlfriend in front of the man, and still he was bringing Trisha gifts? Something was very wrong with this picture. He knew if the situation had been reversed, and he'd caught Sugar sprawled on top of Hallie kissing the hell out of her, he'd have dragged him up by the scruff of the neck and tossed him through a window. Exhaling wearily, he ran a hand over his eyes. "Man, are you sleeping with her or not?"

"Huh?"

Nate met Sugar's befuddled gaze, knowing this wasn't his business, but he had an insane need to know. "Is Hallie your woman or isn't she?"

Sugar's lips lifted wryly. "I don't think you'd rightly call Hallie anybody's woman. She's pretty much her own boss."

"Yeah, well—" Nate shrugged. "That's not exactly news." He turned away and grabbed his doorknob. "Have a good trip."

Something clamped down on his shoulder, and he had a strong suspicion it was Sugar's beefy paw. He swallowed hard. Had it finally sunk in? Was Sugar finally angry? Was he about to get the black eye he deserved? "You kinda like her, ol' buddy?"

Nate shook his head, not in answer, in frustration. "Maybe—kinda," he mumbled, then checked himself. "Hell, *no!* I mean, I don't know." He closed his eyes.

"You want me to guess?"

Nate set his jaw, damning himself for not getting his newspaper five minutes earlier. This conversation was turning him into a blithering idiot. And for a bonus, he'd probably get that black eye any second now.

"Just so we're clear, ol' buddy, when I drop by Hallie's I sleep on the sofa." Sugar took his hand away. "It's the way she wants things."

Nate experienced a run of contradictory emotions. They weren't sleeping together. That was good. On the other hand, Nate couldn't tell from Sugar's tone if the nonsexual status quo was okay with him. That wasn't so good.

If Nate knew men—and being one, he figured he did—no man with a single functioning brain corpuscle would be satisfied with an asexual status quo with Hallie for very long. Resigned, maybe, but never satisfied. Of course the jury was still out on Sugar's brain.

Hallie was a spectacularly sexual being. Who knew what insignificant thing might happen to make that overgrown stud start looking *real* good to her?

Nate wished he hadn't opened this can of worms, but for some demented reason he had to dig in. "You're willing to follow her around like a puppy? Play by her book?"

Sugar's grin was almost shy. "I'd rather have her as a friend than nothin'. She's a good person."

"You don't mind her strong-arming you?"

Sugar readjusted his duffel, then regarded Nate, his expression dubious. "Are we talking about the same

Hallie?'' He scratched his chin, inclining his head toward her door. ''This Hallie here?'' Sugar stared at him as if he'd just grown an extra nose.

Nate frowned, restlessly slapping the newspaper against his thigh. ''She's pushy,'' he finally responded. ''Women like that give me a pain.''

Sugar lifted his chin and peered down his nose at Nate. He seemed to be trying to rev up a thought. ''A pain, huh?'' He squinted, his expression skeptical, or testy, or both. ''If that's how you feel...'' Sugar adjusted his Stetson low on his brow and lumbered toward the stairs. ''Quit kissin' her, ol' buddy.''

THE SUN CAME OUT and granted the world a touch of warmth. On this last day of the year, the temperature nudged into the fifties. The four-inch mantle of snow was melting fast. At one o'clock Nate and Trisha headed out for their daily trek to the supermarket. As he crossed the parking lot, a familiar car pulled to a stop at the exit. He glanced over. It was Hallie.

She rolled down her window. ''Can I give you two a lift?''

Nate heard the reluctance in her voice, saw it in her eyes. Clearly, she was still smarting about last night. He felt like a bum. No matter how she felt about him, she didn't let it stand in the way of being neighborly.

Shoving his hands into his coat pockets, he trudged her way. When he reached the car, he hunched down to see her better. ''Thanks, but Trisha likes our walks.'' He didn't want to add that he'd been avoiding asking her for help. He needed space and time, to get his head on straight.

She nodded. ''Okay.'' When she began to roll up

the window, Nate clamped a hand on the glass, preventing it from going up more than halfway. "Just a second," he said, a fierce inner need gripping him. She glanced up, regarding him with a mixture of anxiety and sadness. He wanted to reach out, touch her face, smooth away the unhappiness he saw there. "Tonight's New Year's Eve, and I was wondering—"

"Sure," she broke in, casting her gaze away.

"You will?" He was astonished that she'd accepted so readily, if not enthusiastically. "Great. I'll pick you up at, say, eight? It's a formal party. I told them I wasn't sure I'd go, but if you'd like, we could still accept. Do you have anything formal?" He was rambling, he knew, and he hated it. But he was stunned that she'd accepted a date with him. His brain was working fast and furiously; he had to get the deal cemented before she changed her mind.

Hallie faced him and his smile vanished when he saw her horrified expression. "What's wrong?"

"I thought you wanted me to baby-sit."

He felt gut-punched. "No..." He sucked in an uneven breath as she stared in disbelief.

"You were asking me out?"

He nodded, his stomach clenching. Her tone made it sound criminal, as if he'd asked her to stick up a gas station or something.

"For New Year's Eve?"

He eyed heaven. "Yeah." What was he supposed to do now? Apologize for asking?

"You're *not* serious."

He couldn't tell by her flickering eyes if she was simply being difficult, or if she was hurt. Why in blazes would she be hurt? They'd barely met until a week ago. How much notice did she expect? No, she couldn't be hurt. She was making it unmistakably clear that she would *not* go out with him, under any circumstances.

Feeling absurdly deflated, he straightened. "I lost my head for a second. Forget it."

"Fine." She clamped her hand on the window handle and rolled, but nothing happened. "Do you mind?" She eyed his fingers, locked over the frame of the open window.

He let go. Running a hand through his hair, he regarded her with high frustration. "Look, Hallie..." He reached toward her in a beseeching gesture, not sure what he planned to do or say.

She stopped rolling up the window and peered at him, her expression skeptical. "What?" The question was clipped, high-pitched, giving him no hope that she had any desire to linger there to hear anything he might say.

The fingers of his outstretched hand curled into a fist and he dropped it to his side. "Nothing." He tried a nonchalant grin, but feared it didn't come off very well. "Thanks for the ride offer."

She lifted one shoulder in a dismissive gesture and rolled the window all the way up.

After she drove away, Nate jammed his hands into his pockets and strode off toward the market. "What is it about that woman that makes me act like a babbling fool?" he mumbled. "What's wrong with your daddy, Trisha?"

Even if his daughter could understand his question, Nate didn't think she'd be much help. He was a grown man and he had never run across this exhilarating, exasperating mix of feelings about any woman before.

Not even Viv.

His ex-wife had idolized him and that had been enough. For a while. Her leaving had been bothersome, but he hadn't been heartbroken.

Then along came Hallie St. John—opinionated, independent, and disturbing on too many levels, one of the most disturbing being that she didn't like him.

Could he blame Hallie? All she'd ever done was try to make sure his daughter was well cared for, and what had he given her in return? A lot of grief, that's what. His only excuse was that he'd gone a little nuts. Since Christmas morning, when she'd confronted him at his door with those damnable, wonderful hazel eyes and dressed in nothing but that flannel nightgown, he hadn't been himself. And then there was Trisha...

He hadn't been able to comprehend how someone so wrong for him could seem so utterly right. But today, for the first time, he was beginning to understand that Hallie had never nagged or harangued or bullied. She'd simply been zealous in her attempts to turn him into at least a fair-to-middling father. He had to admit, considering the number of days, she hadn't done a half-bad job. He was fairly comfortable with Trisha, now. He knew he owed that, to a great extent, to Hallie's strength and her caring nature.

Sadly, in the process of finding out she was quite a woman, he'd alienated himself from her but good. He thought about the Richmonds again, and shook his head. Now—since Hallie—he knew the couple had truly, unselfishly loved each other. So it seemed it *was* possible to have a relationship where two people were equals, each with strengths and weaknesses that could complement and support the other. But was it possible for *him?*

He didn't know. He didn't know if he wanted to try. Maybe he was too bound in the ropes of his family's unhappy history to change his thinking.

Trisha made a cooing sound and he reached back to affectionately squeeze her foot. "Tee, honey?" he said through a troubled exhale. "Do you think you can help Daddy?"

His daughter spouted some gibberish and Nate smiled in spite of himself. There was little hope his four-month-old daughter could give him any sage advice.

11

HALLIE RENTED VIDEOS and shopped a few sales. She picked up a new skirt and slip, but wasn't particularly excited about her purchases. They were just things she needed. All in all, she'd spent the afternoon feeling listless and drained. She chose not to think about why.

It was well after dark by seven o'clock, when she got back to the apartment building. Traffic was picking up as people headed out to New Year's Eve parties. Forcing those thoughts from her mind, she fished in her purse for her key. For the thousandth time today, she experienced a stab of regret about how she'd behaved that afternoon when Nate asked her out.

At first she'd misunderstood, never dreaming he'd meant to ask her for a date. When she realized he had, she was stunned, excited, nervous and frightened, all at once. Yes, she wanted to go. Badly! Her heart had done a high kick that almost threw her off balance in the front seat of her car.

She didn't know how she'd managed, but she'd kept herself from crying out, "Yes! Oh, yes!" Though she was thankful she'd remained strong, she didn't feel good about the way she'd handled it. She'd been downright rude. Why did it have to be that the only choices she had with Nate were to meekly submit to residing under his thumb, or flail like a churlish witch in her effort to maintain her equilibrium?

She continued to grope around in her purse, but had no luck finding her key. Heaving a sigh, she set down her packages and checked her coat pocket. Ah! There it was! Retrieving it, she shoved it into her door just as Nate came out of his apartment.

When their glances clashed, he stopped. She went quivery, her legs turning to mush. In her whole life, Hallie had never seen a man who looked so yummy in a tux, not even on the cover of the slickest men's magazines.

He had a black overcoat thrown across one arm; a white muffler around his neck. He looked casually elegant and all male from the confident set of his wide shoulders to the square cut of his jaw.

His eyes were startlingly pale and compelling within the dark frame of his lashes. His precisely combed hair shone in the mellow hallway light and his handsome face was kindled with such rare, masculine beauty, she found herself unable to catch her breath.

The sight filled her with longing—and alarm. The florist's corsage box he carried inflicted new, bitter damage to her heart.

A muscle flexed in his jaw as he clenched and unclenched his teeth, making it clear he wasn't happy about running into her. Strange. Lately, these chance encounters seemed to happen every day. They'd hardly ever run into each other before Christmas. Fate, it seemed, had a rotten sense of humor.

"Good evening," he said.

His remark snapped her out of her bizarre paralysis and she sucked in a breath. She could detect his scent, subtle and sexy. Oh, how she missed smelling it on her own body. "You going out?" She bit down hard on her tongue. Why hadn't she just shouted, "You're so sexy, my mind is blown. Ignore me and my drool."

His lips twisted in a cynical smile. "I thought I mentioned something about the possibility this afternoon." He leaned a shoulder against the doorframe. "Remember?"

Yes, she remembered! And considering the orchid he held, he'd managed to find another date without difficulty. She battled down a sickening surge of envy. "Oh—right."

She could feel the hot trail of his eyes as he surveyed her from head to toe with uncomfortable thoroughness. She wore jeans, an old, comfortable sweater and her belted peacoat. Nobody's idea of gala New Year's Eve apparel.

"Do you have an exciting evening planned?" he asked.

She turned away, unlocking her door with more violence than necessary. "Absolutely," she lied. "It's gonna rock." Darn him! He knew she didn't have a date! She'd offered to baby-sit, hadn't she? He was being vindictive.

"Rock on, sweetheart," he said to her back, but there was precious little inflection in his voice.

She hurried inside, slamming the door between them. Her lips trembling, she sagged against the wood, fighting tears.

The sudden knock scared her so badly she jumped five feet back. *"What?"* she hollered. "Who's there?"

"Nate."

She pressed a calming hand to her pounding breast and took in a gulp of air. "What do you want?"

"You left your packages out here."

Her packages? Horrified, she checked her empty hands. He was right.

Adjusting her face to mask her unhappiness, she swung the door open. There he stood, the same unimaginably handsome man, holding two department store sacks and a video store bag. Her heart turned over.

Watching her from beneath half-lowered lids, he held them out. "Black lace?" One brow lifted provocatively.

She shot him an indignant look and grabbed the packages. It appalled her to note that her hands shook, making the sacks rattle. "How dare you dig through my stuff!"

His lips tilted slightly at the corners, but the humor in his expression was minimal. "The sack fell over. I put the slip back inside." He slid his hands into his pants' pockets, the move subtly erotic. "You're welcome."

"Hey, there," came a bellow from the direction of the steps. "Happy New Year, ol' buddy! You chattin' with my best gal?"

Nate swiveled toward the trucker, his eyebrows dipping. "I thought you were gone." He sounded as enthused as a man who saw a doctor coming at him with a hypodermic needle. "Welcome back."

Hallie was dumbfounded. She'd thought Sugar would be halfway to Albuquerque by now. She peeked around the door to confirm that it was really him, but didn't dare step out. She'd be too close to Nate.

Her mood lifted at the sight of her burly friend trudging along the hallway. "Sugar?" Having him around would keep her mind off—things. "What are you doing here?"

He tromped toward them, grinning. "Problem with my load. Honcho finally told me to come back tomorrow." He held his arms out in a wide, inviting gesture. "So, darlin', looks like you and me are bringing in the New Year together. How's that sound?"

Hallie was so grateful she wasn't going to be alone, she dumped her bags and hugged his middle. She noticed absently that he smelled like a hamburger, heavy on the onions. "I'm thrilled. We'll ring in this New Year like no New Year's ever been rung in before!" To heck with Nate and his plans with his fluffy Buffy, or whoever! Hallie and Sugar would make spicy cheesy nachos and watch movies. She'd have fun if it killed her!

"Well, that sure does take the kinks out of a man." Sugar guffawed. "I'm up for any old thing you say, darlin'." He winked. Hallie thought she saw a flash of discomfort in Nate's blue eyes. "I see you're going out, ol' buddy," Sugar went on. "You taking some— *nonirritatin'* little gal on the town?"

Nate's jaw shifted from side to side, his nostrils flaring. "Yeah." He eyed Hallie, then glanced back at Sugar.

"Well, have a good one, then." Sugar hugged Hallie to him. "We don't want to keep you." He slapped Nate's back. "You go on now and try to have as good a time as me and Hallie plan to."

Nate didn't immediately move. His gaze flicked over Hallie, snuggled beneath Sugar's arm. He seemed to weigh what he saw with a critical squint.

Hallie was perplexed by both his expression and his hesitation.

"What is it, ol' buddy?" Sugar stroked his five-o'clock shadow. "You got something stuck in your craw?"

Nate skewered Sugar with a hard look. "Not a thing," he muttered, stalking away.

"OKAY, SUGAR..." Hallie pulled her rented tapes from the sack. "I've got *Gone with the Wind, Casablanca, West Side Story* and *Love Story*. What do you want to watch first?"

Sugar plopped down on the couch. Planting his elbows on his knees, he clasped his hands loosely between them. "I don't know." He squinted at the tapes laid out on the coffee table. "What are they about?"

Hallie settled beside him, pointing to each tape. "That one's about a woman who loses the man she loves. That next one's about a woman who loses the man she loves. This one, here, is about a woman who..." She winced, starting to detect a trend here. "Uh...loses the man she loves, and that last one's about a woman who dies, consequently losing the man she loves." She peered at Sugar, a disconcerted blush heating her face. "Your choice."

He snorted. "Why do I get the feeling there's no twenty-car crackups or exploding buildings or slimy aliens in the whole batch?"

Trying to work herself into a better mood for her company, she poked his arm. "Would you believe they were all rented?"

"I'd try real hard."

She grinned, but it wasn't easy. Her melancholy

state seemed to have a mind of its own. "You're a pal."

He cocked his head, eyeing her seriously. "I may not be the smartest cowpoke on the ranch, darlin', but I'm thinkin' you're not in a very good mood tonight."

She had never known Sugar to hit the nail so squarely on the head. Dropping her gaze, she ran her hands through her hair and sighed.

"Uh-huh." With a thoughtful frown, he picked up *Gone with the Wind* and examined it front and back. "I'm wondering what's making you sad."

She shook her head at him. "Nothing worth talking about. Let's skip it, okay?"

"If you say so." With a pitying grimace, Sugar took her hand. "Look, Hallie. I'm crazy about you, you know that." He squeezed her fingers, then let go. "I may be a little slow, but in the last few months I figured out some things. One is that no matter how much I wanted to be, I'm not the right man for you. You need somebody more like you. Smart and strong." He leaned back, putting an arm around her shoulders and squeezing fondly. "You need some guy who'll stimulate your brain." He chuckled. "And I need a woman who likes trashy truck stop stuff."

"Oh, Sugar, it's not—"

He held up his hand. "Hush. You don't think I believe you're crazy for the stuff I bring you, do you? You think it's tacky, but you're a good sport about it." He shook his head, grinning ruefully. "But the thing is, I like it. And there's women out there who do, too." He nodded again, looking away. "She's out there, the woman for me. She's not as smart or as strong as you, but someday I'll run across her. I'm not worried—'bout either of us." He smiled at Hallie and patted her knee. "So, you wanna make nachos?" He stood and held out a hand. "Then, I think I'd like to watch the movie where the gal loses the man she loves."

Hallie accepted his help, grateful for this big sweet lug's friendship. "Perfect choice," she said.

"Oh, one other thing." Sugar aimed her toward the kitchen. "It's about Mr. Christmas Daddy across the hall."

Hallie's throat went dry. Why did Sugar have to bring *him* up? Couldn't she be free of thoughts about the man for five lousy minutes? "What about him?" she asked, apprehensive.

"Funny thing. He's in a bad mood tonight, too."

Mystified, Hallie eyed Sugar. "Huh?"

He patted her shoulder. "Nothin'."

They watched *Casablanca* first. They were three-quarters of the way through *Love Story,* and their third batch of nachos, when a loud knock at Hallie's door caught her in mid-sniffle. Wiping her eyes, she jumped up. "I'll get it."

Sugar waved her off, grabbing a tissue and wiping at his nose. The man was a sentimental fool, it turned out. Hallie couldn't decide which was more entertaining, watching the tearjerkers or watching Sugar blubber.

The rap at her door sounded again. "Coming." Hallie stuffed the tissue into her hip pocket.

When she opened the door, Goldie stood there, her arms full of baby. A heavy diaper bag was slung over one shoulder. "*Oh...*" Goldie cried, "thank goodness you're home. I thought I could handle babysitting for dear Nate, but my perfume injury is causing me all kinds of trouble."

Trisha whimpered, looking as though she was working herself up into a real bawling fit.

"I can't fix a bottle or change a diaper with this silly finger," Goldie explained. "I'm so relieved you're here." She smiled, but her forehead remained furrowed.

Hallie's heart constricted at the sight of Trisha. She'd been keeping her distance as much as possible, but her weakness for both baby and daddy had overcome her that afternoon when she'd offered them a ride. Taking Trisha from Goldie's arms, she stepped back. "Come in and join the party. I'll get her changed and fed."

Goldie hustled in, her anxiety vanishing. "Oh, a New Year's Eve party!" she squealed, sounding like a schoolgirl. "What fun!"

Hallie didn't mind taking care of Trisha. In all honesty, she loved it. While Sugar and Goldie relaxed on the couch, Hallie took charge of the baby, paying more attention to playing with her on the rug than the movies.

Since *West Side Story* was Goldie's favorite, Sugar put that on next.

Once Trisha was tired out from playing, Hallie settled her between two pillows in the middle of her bed, away from the light and noise. She kissed the baby's sweet-smelling forehead and experienced a burst of raw despair. She'd fallen in love with both the Hawksmoors! "Happy New Year, little one," she whispered brokenly, wiping away a tear.

How could it be that in one short week this baby and her father had slipped stealthily into her heart? She wondered dejectedly how many long years she would have to survive before the potent memories of this Christmas holiday faded away.

A high-pitched scream tore her from her thoughts. Panic ricocheting through her, she raced from the bedroom.

SOUTHERN HILLS was a posh, stately country club in the heart of south Tulsa. Svelte, beautiful people whirled on the ballroom's dance floor not far away from Nate and Buffy, who were sitting at a cozy, candlelit table. The exquisitely appointed banquet room was romantically lit by crystal chandeliers.

Many of Tulsa's wealthiest and most influential citizens were in attendance. Nate didn't belong to the club; he was the guest of a client. This party had turned out to be an excellent opportunity for networking and he'd made several new business contacts.

At ten o'clock their host couple left to attend another party, but they insisted that Nate and Buffy stay to enjoy the rest of the evening. Nate had a feeling they left earlier than they might have, able to take only so much information from Buffy about how to achieve the perfect winter tan.

He checked his watch. Eleven-fifteen. Time crawled by. He glanced at Buffy. She watched him, her expression everlastingly expectant. He smiled and she beamed. With an inward wince, he damned himself for calling Buffy at the last minute. He knew it had been a knee-jerk decision, trying to force Hallie from his mind and return to the old status quo.

He was bored to distraction. To make matters worse, he kept imagining Sugar and Hallie ringing in the New Year "like no other New Year has ever been rung in before.'' What in the hell had Hallie meant by that? He could only imagine, and what he imagined had nothing to do with the platonic relationship Sugar had described this morning!

Buffy touched her hair, as though making sure it was still perfect, or possibly still there. She wore it tossed up and caught in a clawlike thing. Thick strands hung in her face and sprouted out of the claw in all directions. Her dress was a neon pink and cut low. She looked sexy and ready. Even so, he kept thinking about another woman, one in jeans and a peacoat—ringing in the New Year with another man—''like no New Year has ever been rung in before.'' He bit back a curse, making himself focus on his date. After all, it wasn't Buffy's fault he was an ass. ''Would you like to dance?'' he asked.

''If you would,'' she said, still beaming.

He had a hard time maintaining his smile. Couldn't the woman state a simple preference? How was he to know if her feet hurt or if she was dying to try out the samba after taking a hundred dollars' worth of lessons unless she gave him some kind of a hint?

''Are you tired, Buffy?''

She touched his hand. ''Are you?''

''No.''

''Neither am I,'' she added hurriedly.

Nate decided to try an experiment. ''Actually, I *am* tired.''

Buffy chewed on her lower lip as though searching for the right answer. ''Me, too. Actually.''

He exhaled. Just as he'd thought. ''Look, Buffy,'' he began, a little testily, ''I don't care one way or the other. If you want to dance, say so.''

She nodded, looking flustered. "Well, I'd love to—if you want."

He smiled at her, but it was more of a stall to count to ten than any happy urge. "I said, I don't care. What do *you* want?" It came out more curtly than he'd meant it to and he could see discomfiture flicker in her eyes. Reining in his temper, he said more gently, "Just tell me what you want."

She opened her purple lips, then closed them. "Whatever you want, Nate. You know that." She smiled, but disquiet rode her features.

"You can't possibly want what I want all the time," he whispered impatiently. "It's not natural. Tell me what *you* want."

She swallowed. "Oh, Nate…" she whimpered.

"Do you *know* what you want?" he asked. "Ever?"

Tears trembled on her lower lashes. He felt like a first class SOB. *That's great, man. Make the woman cry! A little Happy New Year gift from Nate to Buffy!* Taking her hand, he hunched closer. "I'm sorry," he whispered. "Let's dance."

Her expression eased into a tremulous smile. "I'd love to—if you're sure…"

"I'm sure."

As he stood, a waiter came up to him. "Mr. Hawksmoor?"

Nate turned. "Yes?"

"You have an emergency phone call, sir." The waiter nodded toward the exit. "Because of the noise in here, it's better if you take it in the foyer."

His gut tightening, Nate flashed Buffy a look. "Wait here," he commanded, and Buffy didn't move.

Dogging the waiter, he prayed nothing had happened to Trisha. It never occurred to him, when Goldie's hysterical voice came on the line, that it wouldn't be Trisha who was injured. It would be Hallie.

One hundred miles an hour and five minutes later, Nate's sports car swerved into the apartment's parking lot. Not knowing what to do with Buffy, he'd brought her along.

From what he could understand from a hysterical Goldie, Sugar had hit Hallie. What had come over the man? Maybe the status quo finally got the better of him and he'd tried to use force. *Damn bastard.* When Nate got hold of him, he'd give him a little five-finger status quo right in the face!

With his unhappy date in tow, Nate burst into Hallie's apartment, surprised that paramedics weren't there. "Sit someplace," he ordered Buffy without looking at her. His attention was focused on Hallie, lying on the couch, a compress covering her forehead. "My Lord." He rushed to her. "Are you okay? What did that bastard do?" Nate caressed her cheek, noting her hair was wet, as was a good part of her sweater. "What happened, Hallie?"

She opened her eyes and blinked. "Nate?"

He took her hand. "Are you in pain? Can you see okay?"

She nodded. "I'm fine."

She started to sit up, but he pressed her down. "What are you doing? Wait for the ambulance."

She took the compress off her head and Nate could see a purple knot in the middle of her forehead. Brushing his hands from her shoulders she sat up. "Really, I need to—"

Nate eyed Hallie's wound with rising fury. "Where's Sugar?"

Hallie waved toward the kitchen. "He and Goldie..."

That's all Nate heard as he sprinted into the kitchen. Once there, he was taken aback by what he saw. Water sprayed out of a hole where a sink handle should be. Goldie frantically swabbed water off the kitchen floor into a big plastic bowl. She was sopping wet.

Sugar did a bizarre, lumbering dance in front of the sink in his efforts to keep a bucket over the powerful spray, struggling to direct the water down into the sink. His tap dancing seemed more suited to a slapstick Three Stooges' episode. He looked ridiculous, and was doing precious little good.

"What the hell!"

Goldie looked up. "Oh, thank goodness, Nate, dear. Can you help us? We can't keep up with the water!"

"Did anybody try turning it off?"

"Is that possible?" Goldie's face lit up with hope. "It would certainly help."

Nate's fingers itched to take Sugar apart, but for now he merely eyed the man with deadly intent. "Move."

Sugar slipped and slid on wet tiles. He was flushed, his face and hair dripping, his shirt soggy. "I tried to clog it with gum," he wheezed, "but it shot up like a rocket to the moon. Me and Goldie—"

"Move!" Nate shouted, shoving the feckless man aside. "I'll take care of you later."

As Nate bent to get under the sink, he got a face full of water from Sugar's flailing bucket. With a curse, he dropped to a squat. Wiping at his eyes, he opened the doors below the sink. He found the knobs that turned off the water and twisted.

When the gushing stopped, he ducked his head out. "It's off. Now I'd like to know—"

Goldie clapped her rubber-gloved hands to her chest. "Nate, you've saved us! You're an angel, dear boy." She clambered to her feet.

Nate straightened, pushing back his wet hair so it would drip down his neck rather than into his eyes.

Sugar let the bucket clatter into the sink and ran out without a word. Before Nate could break into pursuit, Goldie clasped him in a soggy hug. "We're so grateful. I thought surely we'd drown."

"Where's Trisha?" Nate asked thinly.

Goldie let go. "Sleeping like a..." Her laugh was squeaky and overloud. Nate could tell she was still teetering on the edge of hysteria. "I was going to say sleeping like a baby, silly me." With a dripping towel, she indicated the direction of Hallie's bedroom. "Trisha's fine. Sound asleep." She giggled again, then stunned Nate by bursting into tears. "It was just terrible, Nate, dear. Thank heaven you got here!"

Though Nate eyed the entrance to the living room, he felt he had to comfort Goldie. The little woman had done her best to help in an emergency that hadn't been her fault. He took her into his arms and patted her back. "It's okay. It's over now. You were a great help." Taking her by the upper arms, he pressed her away. "I should go see about Hallie."

At the mention of Hallie's name, Goldie seemed to snap out of her hysterics. "Oh, yes." She sniffed, tugging at her gloves. "She has such a bump!"

Nate didn't wait for Goldie to finish battling the

rubber things off her hands. Pivoting, he stalked into the living room. Sugar sat on the couch beside Hallie, holding her hands. He looked so broken up Nate decided not to kill him outright.

Seething with fury, he headed for the couch. Grabbing Sugar by his shirtfront, he yanked him up. "You—piece of..." He slammed a vicious, pile-driving fist into the trucker's nose. Caught off guard, Sugar stumbled backward and fell on his butt. Coming up on one elbow, he shook his head as though clearing his vision.

"What do you think you're doing, Nate!" Hallie vaulted up. "How dare you!" She rushed to kneel by Sugar's side. "Did he hurt you?"

Sugar felt his nose. "I think—I'll live."

"You poor thing." Hallie ran a comforting hand along his cheek and glared at Nate. "Are you *insane?*"

Crazed by jealousy as Hallie defended her assailant, Nate felt his rage become a living, breathing entity. "Am *I* insane?" he demanded. "The man punched you! How can you defend him?"

Hallie stared, her face crimson with indignation. "Punched me?"

The incredulous way she repeated those two words gave Nate pause. "Didn't he?"

Sugar straightened, casting a regretful glance at Hallie. "With the bucket." He looked at Nate, his expression full of remorse. "It was an accident. Everything was happening so fast. Water was going everywhere. I didn't see her."

Nate could picture the whole cartoon now. Of course it was an accident. He should have known Sugar would never hurt Hallie on purpose. What was wrong with him? He felt like a worm. "Hell," he muttered, extending a hand toward Sugar. "I'm damn sorry, man."

Sugar grinned wryly, clamping his hand around Nate's. "I figure I'd have done the same thing, ol' buddy. In your place, that is." With Nate's help, Sugar stood. He sniffed, and Nate realized the trucker's nose was bleeding. Renewed guilt washed over him.

"You poor man," came a familiar voice from behind Nate. Buffy appeared. Nate had forgotten all about her. Pulling a tissue from the box on the coffee table, the buxom blonde walked to the big trucker. "Here." She smiled at him. "I've heard ice helps bloody noses." She took his big paw in her tanned little hand and led him toward the kitchen.

"Well…" Goldie exhaled loudly. "If you folks will excuse me, I think I'll take Trisha and *Gone with the Wind* upstairs, change into some dry clothes and party on."

When nobody responded, Goldie cleared her throat. "And why don't I keep the baby all night. Yes. I think I will." Seconds later she and a sleeping Trisha were gone.

Nate's gaze remained locked with Hallie's.

12

HALLIE'S HEAD THROBBED as she glared at Nate. She was furious, but it was difficult to stay that way. His black tie was undone. His formal shirt stuck to his chest, showing off contoured muscle. His hair, which had been perfect a few hours earlier, was mussed and sparkled with water droplets. His eyelashes twinkled as though they held a treasure trove of diamonds. And he looked vulnerable, unsure of himself.

She tried to bolster her animosity. *He hit Sugar!* There was no excuse for such uncalled-for violence.

"I know," he said quietly, "I'm a pig."

She lifted her chin. "At least."

He inhaled, his expression repentant. A drop of water escaped his hairline and skidded down his forehead to melt into his lashes. He blinked, freeing the droplet to trail to the edge of his sharp cheekbone and shimmer there. "What do you want me to do?" he asked.

"Fix my sink," she said. "You are my landlord, remember?"

He looked away, then met her gaze again, his blue eyes watchful. "I guess it's the least I can do."

"I repeat, *at least.*"

He nodded, shrugging off his damp tux jacket. "I'll get some tools." He rolled up his shirtsleeves, revealing sturdy forearms. Discarding his tie, he opened his shirt collar.

Not too many minutes later Hallie found herself helping Nate fix the faucet handle. She tried to convince herself she did it grudgingly, because it was her apartment. But that wasn't the reason and she knew it.

Somewhere during it all, Hallie became aware that Sugar and Buffy were gone. Hallie thought she'd heard Buffy giggle and say something about showing Sugar her snow globe collection. But the whereabouts of those two was the least of her worries at the moment.

Every so often she caught a glimpse of Nate's hips as she bent to get him a screwdriver or to put a wrench away, and her heart fluttered madly. She remembered the feel of those hips under her fingers. Firm. Warm. She recalled his birthmark. Her wayward gaze lingered on the spot where it resided for long painful seconds before she managed to look away. Unfortunately, her thoughts tarried.

"It's done," he said at last, and their eyes met.

She nodded, no longer able to conjure up a single molecule of anger.

She'd already mopped up the rest of the water, so the kitchen was definitely on the mend. The only problem was her bathroom. The tub and shower stall held every towel she owned. Filthy and sopping. Until she could get them washed, her bathroom was of little use to her. And even if it were, she had no clean, dry towels. Avoiding his eyes, she stooped to close the toolbox. Before she could reach it, Nate grasped her elbow and coaxed her to stand.

"What is it?" she asked, confused.

"It's midnight." Something glinted deep in his eyes.

She experienced a slight, watchful hesitation, but no words came.

"I have to kiss you," he murmured. "It's tradition."

Uneasiness spiced with anticipation dashed along her spine. She shifted restlessly, not sure how to respond. She couldn't deny that she craved the feel of his lips against hers, but she knew that allowing herself such an erotic indulgence would be playing with fire.

She instructed her head to shake from side to side in the negative, and she instructed her tongue to say no. She waited for all this to happen. It didn't. Instead, a tiny sound of longing issued up from her throat.

Nate heard it because he smiled and dipped his head toward her. She tried desperately to conjure up some unmistakable sign of rejection. A push, a sharp word, a damning look. *Anything!* But all her efforts were in vain. Her unbidden love for him overrode her good sense and she tilted her chin in invitation. "Tradition," she whispered, calling herself every kind of fool.

He kissed her and it was like the touch of heaven. So whisper-light she had a flash of panic that he would pull away. Her arms flew around his neck to stop any retreat. She kissed him back, suddenly breathless, urgent. A sound of wonder came from his throat, and he tugged her against him. Once again, she knew the feel of heaven. His scent surrounded her, sailed into her lungs, made her quiver with renewed longing.

Losing her mind, she allowed one hand to slide down, cupping his hip. With a heady inhale, she relished the delicious, hard feel of him. He lifted his lips slightly away from hers. "Oh, Lord—Hallie..." His voice was husky, full of sexy promise. "Yes, this is right...."

Her eyes popped open. What was right? Sex with Nate? It felt right, that was true. But it wasn't right! He wanted a meek woman!

"No—no—no!" she cried. "Let me go!" Her limbs were shaky and too feeble to free her from his arms.

He inched his face back, gazing at her in disbelief. "But, Hallie..."

She pressed hard, tears welling. "Let me go, Nate!"

When he did, she lurched away, shouting, "I need a shower." She slammed into her bathroom and was met with the havoc she'd momentarily forgotten. She couldn't take a shower in here. Pressing her fists to her temples, she squeezed her eyes tight, trying not to scream in frustration.

Slamming back out, she got as far as the living room. But when she saw Nate standing there she stopped abruptly. They stared at each other. He looked troubled, sad, angry. His eyes flashed, a muscle in his cheek flexed. Well, if he was angry, he could just join the club!

She heaved a moan. "I can't take a shower in there! There's no room for me and I don't have any towels." Why a few wet towels sent her over the edge, she didn't know. But all of a sudden it was too much to bear, and she burst into shuddery sobs. Covering her face with shaky hands, she let herself cry, not caring that he was watching. She was too far gone to hold her tattered emotions in check one second longer.

He took her into his arms. "Don't cry. You can use my shower."

She wanted to slip her arms around his neck and hold on—forever. But she couldn't be his little Buffy clone. She wouldn't be any man's slave! "I'm not crying!" Running the back of her hand across her nose, she avoided his eyes. "I should think you would offer me your shower," she retorted, trying for emotional distance. "You owe me, buster."

"Yeah," he said softly. She didn't dare look at his face. His quiet acceptance made her realize her emotional-distance plan wasn't working. She had to pump up the voltage. Make him want to keep his distance, because she knew she was lost. If he held out his arms, she'd fall into them—his groveling slave.

Bucking up, she turned her back. A safeguard measure to make sure her gaze didn't drift helplessly to his. "I'm hungry," she stated. "I have a taste for pancakes and good, strong coffee." Tromping toward the door, she added, "I'll take my shower while you fix it."

Hurrying to his bathroom, she peeled off her wet things and jumped into the shower stall. Under the pulsating stream, she let her sobs come freely. She loved Nate, but they wanted totally opposite things in their mates. This was the best way. A clean break! She was positive when she got out of the shower Nate would be out of her life.

A grim realization intruded and she cringed. This was Nate's apartment! She was using his shower! She slumped against the cool tile wall, feeling defeated.

What was worse, she hadn't remembered to bring a stitch of clothes to change into! Was her ultimate disgrace to be marched naked to his door, and then kicked unceremoniously out on her bare backside? She squeezed her eyes shut, trying to block out the vision. "Well," she mumbled, "no matter how degrading he makes the experience, at least it will be over once and for—"

A creaking noise told her the shower door was opening. A new, horrible picture slammed into her brain. He's going to dump pancake mix and coffee on my head!

Before she could throw up her arms in self-defense, Nate stepped in. Gloriously naked, he took her in his arms.

She gasped. "What are you doing?"

He grinned, smoothing hair back from her face and kissing her temple. "I thought we could both take a shower, then make breakfast together."

She stared in mute shock. This wasn't humiliating or humbling or punishing—unless he planned to taunt her with something she longed for but could never have again. Too confused to take any action, she simply kept on staring.

His smile dimmed but his eyes glistened with warmth and love. "Hallie, I figured out something. Do you want to know what?"

Trying to get a grip on what was happening, she nodded dumbly.

"I figured out that it's not necessary to have one weakling in every relationship."

She blinked and he chuckled. She felt his laughter in places she'd never felt laughter before. The sensation made her weak and she lifted her hands to his shoulders for support. At least, that's what she told herself she was doing. "I—I don't understand," she whispered.

"Emotionally stable people don't have to dominate their mates." He tenderly kissed the skin beside her bruise. "I watched my mother all those years, and I know she wasn't a happy person. All her domineering and bossing didn't give her contentment. I figure you found that out about your father, too."

Hallie nodded, dazed. What was he saying?

"You're a strong, stubborn woman, Hallie St. John." He kissed the skin on the other side of her bruise. "I love the hell out of you."

Love? He loved her? She couldn't believe her ears. "But…but I thought you wanted a submissive woman."

He chuckled again, and Hallie went all warm and gooey inside.

"I thought so, too," he murmured, "but damned if you didn't prove me wrong."

She cocked a dubious brow. "You? *Wrong?*"

Reaching for the soap, he began to massage along her shoulder. "My parents' marriage was a dysfunctional mess. My brother's marriage is a dysfunctional mess." He spoke slowly, as though feeling his way. "I promised myself I'd be smarter, but I made a mess of my first marriage because I tried so hard not to end up like my dad. I did it wrong."

He soaped along her collarbone, then lower, over the rise of a breast, caressing, arousing. "You helped me understand what a healthy relationship is. Your father and my mother were selfish people, Hallie. We don't have to be. We've seen it done wrong. I think we're smart enough, and we want it badly enough, to do it right—together.'' He dipped his head, tasting her lips. ''Will you marry me?''

Her heart fluttered with hope, but she had lived so long with the pain and fear of being dominated, she couldn't let herself believe him. Not just like that! ''What if I say no?'' she asked breathlessly, wanting him, wanting it, but not daring to dream.

''Then I'll ask again.''

''No ordering?''

''Only in restaurants.'' His expression was tender, earnest.

The massaging moved lower, becoming erotic, and Hallie moaned with pleasure. ''W-what if we disagree?''

''I'll try not to pass out in surprise,'' he teased, kissing one corner of her mouth, then the other. ''Please. Marry me, Hallie.''

With soul-deep certainty, she knew he truly meant it. Her heart overflowing with joy, she surrendered to his gentle coaxing, pressing into him, rubbing seductively. ''I'll make the coffee,'' she whispered. ''You're better at pancakes.''

''Is that a yes?''

Touched by the emotion in his voice, Hallie's heart burst with a new, overwhelming happiness. Slipping a teasing hand over his chest, she said, ''I need more soap.''

His brows quirked in surprise, but quickly reading her smirk, his eyes twinkled with promise. ''Why don't I do it for you?''

She smiled playfully. ''You'd do that for me?''

His grin wicked, he lathered his hands, then put the soap away. His erotic touch made her gasp with delight. ''I want to make you happy, darling.''

Slowly, seductively fanning the sparks of arousal into flame, he made Hallie wildly happy, and was rewarded with the yes he hoped for—breathlessly cried out over and over and over.

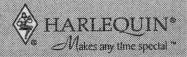

Take 2 bestselling love stories FREE

Plus get a FREE surprise gift!

Special Limited-Time Offer

Mail to Harlequin Reader Service®

3010 Walden Avenue
P.O. Box 1867
Buffalo, N.Y. 14240-1867

YES! Please send me 2 free Harlequin Love & Laughter™ novels and my free surprise gift. Then send me 4 brand-new novels every other month, which I will receive months before they appear in bookstores. Bill me at the low price of $2.90 each plus 25¢ delivery per book and applicable sales tax if any*. That's the complete price, and a saving of over 10% off the cover prices—quite a bargain! I understand that accepting the books and gift places me under no obligation ever to buy any books. I can always return a shipment and cancel at any time. Even if I never buy another book from Harlequin, the 2 free books and the surprise gift are mine to keep forever.

102 HEN CH7N

Name	(PLEASE PRINT)	
Address	Apt. No.	
City	State	Zip

This offer is limited to one order per household and not valid to present Love & Laughter™ subscribers. *Terms and prices are subject to change without notice. Sales tax applicable in N.Y.

**WHEN THINGS START TO HEAT UP
HIRE A BODYGUARD...**

AND THEN IT GETS HOTTER!

There's a bodyguard agency in San Francisco where
you can always find a HERO FOR HIRE, and the man
of your sexiest fantasies.... Five of your favorite
Temptation authors have just been there:

JOANN ROSS *1-800-HERO*
August 1998
KATE HOFFMANN *A BODY TO DIE FOR*
September 1998
PATRICIA RYAN *IN HOT PURSUIT*
October 1998
MARGARET BROWNLEY *BODY LANGUAGE*
November 1998
RUTH JEAN DALE *A PRIVATE EYEFUL*
December 1998

HERO FOR HIRE
A blockbuster miniseries.

Available at your favorite retail outlet.

◆HARLEQUIN®

Temptation®

Not The Same Old Story!

Exciting, glamorous romance stories that take readers around the world.

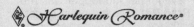
Sparkling, fresh and tender love stories that bring you pure romance.

Bold and adventurous— Temptation is strong women, bad boys, great sex!

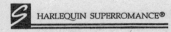
Provocative and realistic stories that celebrate life and love.

Contemporary fairy tales—where anything is possible and where dreams come true.

Heart-stopping, suspenseful adventures that combine the best of romance and mystery.

Humorous and romantic stories that capture the lighter side of love.

LOVE & LAUGH

INTO JANUARY!

#59 THE HIJACKED BRIDE
Liz Ireland
Bride-to-be Cathy Seymour refused to let abduction stop her marriage plans—even if her kidnapper was the hunkiest guy this side of Brad Pitt. She intended to get back to her stable, banker fiancé, Bob, no matter what his brother, Hale Delaney—her kidnapper—claimed about Bob's supposed *criminal* activities. So why was the awesomely sexy kidnapper looking better by the second…?

#60 HOME IMPROVEMENT
Barbara Daly
Interior decorator Sunny O'Brien was in a bad fix: she'd lost her New York apartment, and her Vermont cottage was falling down about her ears. So she hired Colin Blalock, a man who despised her fast-paced life and her desire to sell the cottage and return to New York. He was also gorgeous, devoted to his family and the best darn kisser Sunny had ever met. But she wanted city not country…didn't she?

Chuckles available now:

#57 GIFT-WRAPPED BABY
Renee Roszel
#58 NAUGHTY OR NICE?
Stephanie Bond

LOVE & LAUGHTER™